TEMPTED BY THE CEO

EMILY HAYES

1

OLIVIA

"Liv. You're doing it again."

Olivia Jones glanced up at her father, grinning sheepishly. "I know. Just ten more minutes."

"You know, when I told you that you'd have to work hard as CEO, I didn't mean you should work yourself into a nervous breakdown."

"I'm not having a nervous breakdown, Dad."

"Not yet," he muttered.

"Relax. Just ten more minutes and I'll be done."

Kane narrowed his eyes suspiciously. "I'll wait for you."

Shoot. There was no way Liv was staying much later. "Fine. I'll see you in ten minutes."

It was just two months since her father had promoted her to CEO, and it was a lot of work. He kept pushing her to maintain boundaries between work and her personal life, but Liv couldn't help it that she loved her job.

She had helped him raise Aimee Enterprises from the ground up. The had started off as a small, struggling business, but they had grown into one of the most successful companies in the transport industry.

She was invested in their success, to say the least. When her mother, Aimee, died, Liv and her father got through it by leaning on each other, bringing them closer than they had ever been before. Liv knew that it was unusual for an adult daughter to be living with her father still, but she didn't care about what other people thought. They were both happy with the way things were.

Unfortunately, she knew that her father was right. She *did* need to work on allocating herself more free time.

So, after ten minutes, she regretfully closed the folder she was working on and got up. Kane was waiting for her.

"Let's go out to dinner tonight."

They usually had dinner at home after a long

day, saving nights out for weekends, but Liv wasn't opposed to the idea. "Sure. Joe's Diner?"

"Exactly what I was thinking." Liv had a weakness for cheese burgers. She made up for it with going to the gym every morning before work, but she knew that it wasn't exactly healthy, no matter how much time she spent working out.

Stacy zeroed in on them the moment they walked into the diner. She knew that they were regulars who were always polite and tipped well.

"Hey Kane, Liv. The usual, I take it?"

"Please, Stacy. Olivia?"

"The same for me as well."

Stacey bustled off to get their order ready while Kane looked out of the window.

"Everything ok, Dad? You seem tense."

He sighed. "You know me too well. It's... well, I have news."

"Oh yeah?" 'News' could mean something good or bad, and Liv couldn't help but worry. Was she not doing a good job as CEO? The company profits were at a record high, employee satisfaction was rated at nine and a half out of ten, and Liv was working as hard as she'd promised. Still, perhaps her father thought differently.

His voice brought her out of her anxious thoughts. "I proposed to Laura."

"Oh!" That wasn't what she'd been expecting. "Did she say yes?"

"She did."

Liv leaned over the table to hug him. "I'm happy for you, Dad. I know how much you love her."

"She'll be moving in with us."

Liv should have expected that, but the words sent a tingle of nerves though her. "Are you sure she'll... be ok? With me, I mean?"

Liv liked Laura, but she had one fatal flaw – she was homophobic. She wasn't passionately and outwardly bigoted like some people were, but she still held the private belief that being gay was wrong. In the early days of the relationship, Liv and Kane had fought about it a lot.

Liv hadn't been able to believe that he'd date a homophobe, knowing that his daughter was gay. It had taken her some time to even agree to meet Laura, but when she had, she realized that Laura was far from the monster she had thought her to be.

"She'll be fine, Liv. You know she's trying. She can't help it that she was brought up in a very conservative religious household. She likes you and she's already made great progress toward correcting her beliefs. She's just not quite there yet. We need to be patient with her."

Liv knew that he was right about Laura changing; she had seen that change herself. However, Laura still held onto some unsavory beliefs, and that didn't sit right with Liv. It had never come up between the two of them, but if they were living together...

"Stop worrying. I've made myself clear to Laura from the start. The moment she shows any form of bigoty toward you – even one negative comment – and we're over. That still holds. I love her, but I won't stand for my daughter being made uncomfortable about who she is, especially in her own home."

That was reassuring to hear. Liv was still nervous, but in the end, she trusted her dad's judgment. "Well, hopefully living with me will help convince her that I'm not really that different to anyone else other than in who I choose to love."

"Exactly. She was brought up to believe that gay people are immoral, but living right alongside you will show her that your ethics aren't far away from hers."

"I'm sure we can make it work." She had to, for her dad's sake. He was deeply in love with Laura, and Liv wanted him to be happy. It had been so many long years since Liv's beloved mom had died and they had both been through so much grief. He deserved some happiness finally and Laura did make him happy.

"There's one other thing. Her daughter, Juliette, will be moving in with her."

Oh.

Liv knew that Laura had a daughter, but she hadn't met her before. This was something she couldn't have expected. They had plenty of room in the house. Kane and Aimee had been planning on having more children when Aimee died, and they had never moved out of their luxurious and spacious four-bedroom home.

Space wasn't the issue, though.

"Are you sure that's a good idea? Bringing two people into the house... I don't want what we have to change."

Liv valued her dynamic with her father highly, and she would hate for someone else to come in and mess it up.

"Nothing is going to change. Juliette is great, you'll see. I'm sure you'll all get along just fine, and it's not like we won't get our one-on-one time anymore. We still work together, and we'll still go out for lunch or dinner just the two of us sometimes."

"Yes, but a lot more of our activities will be group ones with Juliette and Laura. I like Laura, but I've never even met Juliette."

"True, but they don't have to be. If you don't like Juliette, you don't have to spend time with her. You're both adults. You can figure out how to live together without being friends. That being said, I think you'll like her a lot."

Her father did have good judgment – Liv had seen that many times first hand. For now, she would trust him in this. There was no point in going into this with a closed mind.

"Then I guess I'd better meet this Juliette."

"You'll meet her soon. If you're on board, they'll start moving in next week."

"I'm on board. I'm happy to give this a chance... but Dad, if things don't work out, I may want to get my own place."

"I wouldn't want to chase you out of your own home."

"I wouldn't ask you to live separately from your wife. I know you're wanted to live together for a while, but have been holding off for my sake. I'm a big girl – I can handle it. I'll try my hardest to make it work, but if it comes down to it, I'll be the one who leaves. I'm not letting you sacrifice your happiness for my sake."

"I don't want you to have to sacrifice your happiness for me, either."

"I won't be. I love living with you, but it's not like we wouldn't see each other if I moved out. It would be a change, but I'm sure we could manage it."

"Let's hope it doesn't come to that."

Liv suspected that the success or failure of this venture would depend on how well she and Juliette got along. Laura knew better than to be bigoted toward Liv. Kane wasn't bluffing when he said he'd leave her the moment she was.

Did Juliette hold her mother's beliefs? Even if she didn't, that didn't mean she and Liv would get along. Juliette could be a perfectly lovely person, but that didn't mean they were compatible to live together. Living with someone was intense, and it took some type of natural connection as well as determination to make it work in order to sustain long term.

"Is… does Juliette hold the same beliefs as Laura?"

Kane snorted. "Absolutely not – they're polar opposites in that regard. Half of the progress Laura has made in that area has been thanks to Juliette."

"She's gay as well?"

"No, she's straight, but she's a passionate ally. Some of her best friends are gay. You may have even seen her at pride." Kane chuckled. "You should see the scoldings Laura gets sometimes. Juliette is religious as well, and every time her mother tries to play that card, Juliette plays it right back at her. After all, Jesus taught love and acceptance for everyone, and Laura doesn't really have any argument against that. Poor woman doesn't stand a chance."

Well, that was certainly encouraging. If that was Juliette's attitude, her chances of getting on with Liv increased exponentially.

"It sounds like I need to meet this Juliette."

"I'm sure you'll get along just fine, Liv. Trust me, this is going to be great."

Juliette was nervous. How could she not be? Her mother's happiness depended on this move working, and Juliette wasn't sure it would.

She wasn't worried that she would be the one to ruin things. She had already met Kane and they got along just fine. She hadn't met Olivia before, but she had heard a lot about her from Kane, and Juliette was confident that they would easily become friends.

No, her anxiety was about her mother. Juliette knew that Olivia was gay, and Laura still held onto a few unsavory beliefs about gay people.

If she slipped up so much as once, made even

one homophobic comment or gesture toward Liv, Kane would leave her. He would be right to, but Laura would still be heartbroken.

"Remember, you have to treat Olivia just like you would anyone else."

"I *know*, Juliette, how many times do you have to tell me? I like Liv, even if she is..."

"That. Right there. Comments like that – even ones you cut off before you say something unforgivable – have to go. Liv is a whole person, and being gay is part of that person. If you truly want to be a Christian, then you have to be like Christ, which means loving your neighbor wholly and completely."

Laura pressed her lips together, no doubt holding back the Leviticus verses that were dying to escape.

"I do love Liv."

"If you don't love all of her, that's not good enough. You need to be prepared for the fact that living with her will be different. I know Kane said she's not with anyone right now, but that will most likely change at some point. She will date women. She will bring women home. You're going to have to learn to be ok with gay sex happening down the hall from you. Not only will you treat Liv right, but you will treat her partners right. If you can't do that, then your marriage with Kane is doomed from the start."

"Surely, she doesn't have to do it in the house. I mean, I accept that she's going to do it, but could she not do it somewhere else?"

Juliette took a deep breath, trying to be patient, reminding herself that Laura was trying to overcome an entire lifetime of negative conditioning.

"Would I ask you and Kane to leave your own home every time you wanted to be intimate?"

"That's not the same."

"Yeah, it is. We're moving in today. Get your shit together, mom."

"Don't you talk to me like that, young lady."

"I'll talk to you like this until you act in a way that warrants otherwise. You do want this to work, don't you?"

Laura took a deep breath of her own. "I do. You're right. I need to get my head around this. Gay sex, potentially happening in my home. Yep. I can handle that. I can."

Juliette hoped for her mother's sake that she was right. "It's not wrong," Juliette repeated for emphasis. "Remember what Jesus said."

"Love your neighbor."

"Not love your neighbor conditionally."

Laura nodded. "Yes. Unconditional love. I need to love all of her, even if I find it –"

"Nuh-uh. You stop right there. You need to love all of her. Just leave it at that."

"Ok. Yeah, you're right. As usual. I *will* get my head around this. Gay sex... just like normal sex, right? Different parts don't make any difference. As long as it's between consenting adults, there's no problem."

"Exactly. See? You're learning. I know it's hard for you, mom. It's not your fault you were raised this way, but that doesn't mean you can't take responsibility and put in the effort to change. Now, do you have the flag?"

Laura grimaced. "I still feel like it's hypocritical. I mean, I do love Liv, but this seems like a gift under false pretenses."

"It's important that you show her support, even if you're still working on making that support more sincere. You said yourself – you love her, and I know you *want* to support her, even though you're finding full acceptance hard at the moment. This will show her – and Kane – that you're really trying."

"I am trying. I do want this to work." Laura

pulled a small wrapped package out of her bag. "I hope she likes it."

"Trust me, she will. Support – especially from people close to them – means just as much to queer folks as it does to everyone else."

When she found out they would be moving with Liv, Juliette had dragged Laura out of the house to go shopping for a lesbian pride flag. Laura had resisted at first, but she had allowed Juliette to convince her, like she usually did.

Juliette knew that deep down, Laura knew that her beliefs were wrong. That's why she always allowed Juliette to scold her like a child, and listened attentively whenever Juliette spoke about queer issues. She was sure that with time, her mother would come around.

"Then let's go. We've got a lot of boxes to move."

They made the first trip from the truck to Kane and Liv's house. Juliette grabbed a box of books, hoisted it into her arms and started down the driveway.

Kane and Liv were waiting to meet them. Olivia was slightly blocked by the angle, but as they rounded the corner, Juliette caught a full glimpse of her.

Olivia Jones. *Phew.*

She dropped the box of books, which landed painfully on her toe.

"Fuck! Ow!"

Olivia was suddenly already there, lifting the box of books up. "Here, sit down. Take off your shoe. Let me look at it."

Juliette gaped at her like an idiot. Olivia, Liv was... well, Liv was stunning. Juliette didn't think she'd ever met a woman so beautiful, with short wavy honey-colored hair. She was curvy in all the right ways, and her green eyes seemed to see into Juliette's soul.

Liv wore tight pants and a black button down shirt. Her green eyes fixed Juliette intensely.

"Juliette? Are you alright?"

"I – um. Yes. I'm fine."

"Can you sit down?"

Juliette flopped down onto the bottom stair by the front door.

"May I take your shoe off?"

Juliette nodded dumbly.

Liv gently removed her shoe and examined her foot. "Ok, it doesn't seem to be broken, but you'll have one hell of a bruise. I'll get you an ice pack."

Juliette felt her face burning with embarrassment. What a way to make a good first impression on her soon to be step-sister. Why did Liv have to be so beautiful and clearly confident and capable? It wasn't fair. Juliette had seen beautiful women before, but she had never found herself so totally tongue-tied around them.

Liv went into the house and returned with an ice pack. She placed it gently on Juliette's foot. Juliette knew that Liv was a CEO, not a doctor, and wondered what knowledge Liv was working from.

"Do you have any medical training?"

"When I got promoted to CEO, I got myself certified in advanced first aid. If someone runs into trouble in the office, I want to be able to help."

"Makes sense." Juliette gritted her teeth as she tried to move her toe. It certainly felt like it was broken, but she wasn't certified in first aid, so she would trust Liv's judgment.

"Come on, let's get you inside. You need to elevate this."

Juliette felt her face burning as Liv got her to her feet and pulled one of Juliette's arms over her shoulder. "I'm fine – I can manage."

"Let me help you."

"You can put her on the couch." Kane was there too, witnessing her humiliation. Laura fluttered anxiously as Liv towed Juliette into the house.

"Do you need painkillers?" Laura asked.

"Um... yes please."

Laura rushed off into one of the bathrooms and came back with a first aid kit. She rummaged around until she came up with some Tylenol. Juliette swallowed it gratefully and let Liv help her onto the couch.

Liv's hand was on her lower leg again. "Are you cold?" she asked, her voice silky and smooth, her accent indefinable.

Juliette wasn't cold at all. In fact, she felt quite hot, but everywhere Liv touched her, goosebumps were rising on her skin. How the hell was she supposed to explain that to Liv, though, when she couldn't even explain it to herself?

"I'm fine. Just sore."

"Here, put it up on these cushions."

Juliette did as she was told, lying back and allowing Liv to position the ice pack on her swollen, bruised toe. As she leaned over, her cleavage was exposed in her low shirt. Juliette's mouth went dry.

What the hell was wrong with her? She was

straight, for fuck's sake! Why would she even *care* about another woman's cleavage?

Fortunately, her toe chose that moment to give a particularly painful throb, distracting her from the issue.

Liv cut up a compression bandage to size and carefully wrapped up Juliette's toe. "Thank you," Juliette mumbled. "I'm sure I'll be fine to help again in a few minutes."

"Absolutely not." Kane came over with a glass of water. "You'll stay right there until the swelling goes down. The three of us can handle things."

Juliette felt awful that her blunder meant that she wouldn't be able to help. It hardly made a good impression, lying here on the couch while her new stepfather and stepsister did all the work.

"I suppose we should get back to it." Liv glanced at Juliette again. "You keep that ice pack on for twenty minutes, then off for twenty, then on for another twenty."

Juliette glanced at her watch. "Alright. Thank you, Liv."

"Anytime."

Juliette gave her mother a meaningful look, who hurried forward, taking the wrapped package out of her bag. "Liv, I, uh, I got this for you. I just wanted you to know that I support you."

Juliette could tell that Laura was trying hard not to add a qualifier to that statement. Thankfully, Laura won that battle and handed over the flat.

Liv's face lit up as she unfolded the flag. "Laura – thank you! You don't know how much this means to me."

She pulled Laura into a tight hug.

"I love you, Liv." Laura sounded more sincere this time around. "I want you to be happy, with whoever makes you happy."

It was left unsaid that Juliette's mom would be a lot more comfortable should it be a man making Liv happy. Juliette was sure that Liv and Kane could sense the cut-off statements and careful wording, but neither of them called her out on it. She was trying, and that's what counted. Juliette was glad that Liv at least seemed willing to be patient with Laura's journey.

For the next several hours, Juliette lay guiltily on the couch, trying her best not to stare at Liv. She failed miserably, and the more she looked, the harder it became to look away. She was sure that Liv caught her watching, but Liv seemed to be watching her right back.

At least Liv had good reason. She was into women. Juliette wondered momentarily if Liv was attracted to her. She found the idea strangely alluring. She told herself it was just because it was a compliment, even if the attraction wasn't returned.

And it definitely wasn't returned.

Was it?

Nope. Juliette wasn't going to go down that road. She was straight and that was the end of it.

When they got to unpacking Juliette's paintings, she hauled herself off the couch, pleased to find that her toe wasn't throbbing nearly as badly as before.

"Let me do that."

"Juliette, you should be resting that toe –"

"No, Liv, let her be. My daughter is very fussy about her artwork."

"Oh! I didn't know you're an artist. May I see?"

Juliette was suddenly self-conscious. She wasn't usually shy about her work, but the idea of Liv seeing it made her all tingly with anxiety.

"Um. Sure. I'm not sure if it'll be to your taste. It's pretty abstract."

"I love abstract!"

Juliette took a couple of pieces into the room

that was to be her studio and carefully pulled away the cloth covers.

Liv gasped and took a step forward. "I've seen these before! At least, I've seen ones like them. You go under Julie?"

"It's my little artist nickname." Juliette glanced at her small signature at the bottom of the paintings.

"I've had my eye on one of your pieces for a while. The one with all blues and greens – it reminds me of the ocean. Is that one ever going to be put up for sale?"

Juliette was stunned. She had hoped Liv would like her work, but hadn't imagined she would be a pre-existing fan. "I was actually planning to keep that one."

Liv's face fell. Juliette felt flattered that Liv really liked her work. She loved that piece too, but Liv was basically family now- her new stepsister.

"But if you really like it, you can have it."

"No, no, I'm happy to buy it from you." Liv's face was beautiful and her green eyes were earnest. Juliette didn't want to charge Liv for the painting.

"Please, take it as a gift. I can bring it over tomorrow."

Liv squealed and threw her arms around Juliette. "Thank you! That'll be amazing. You must let me take you out to lunch, to say thank you."

Juliette was hardly going to object to spending more time with Liv. Not only was Juliette somehow fascinated and inspired by Liv's lovely face, but she was so warm and genuine, it was impossible not to like her.

"I'd love that. But perhaps for now, we should finish the unpacking?"

"Right. Yeah, of course."

They unpacked until the sun started to set, making several trips back and forth between the houses. When they were done, all the boxes were at least here, but it would take some time yet to finish unpacking them all.

"Come on, I'll show you to your room."

Kane and Laura watched as Liv led Juliette away, clearly thrilled that their daughters were getting on so well.

When Liv showed her the room, Juliette dug through one of the boxes and found her own pride flag – the ally flag, black and white stripes with a rainbow triangle on top.

Liv didn't say anything, but Juliette saw her grinning as she affixed the flag to her wall.

"I'll get you some bedding."

Juliette was exhausted, and as soon as Liv got her the bedding, she crawled into bed. She was asleep almost instantly.

The next few days were filled with unpacking. Liv, Kane and Laura all had nine-to-five jobs, but Kane and Laura had taken a couple of days off to help. Juliette was touched when Liv did the same, leaving her assistant to handle things and call her if there was an emergency at work.

Judging by Kane's wide-eyed look of surprise, taking time off wasn't something Liv did often.

It didn't seem to escape their respective parents' notice that Liv and Juliette were choosing boxes in the same room to unpack more than would be dictated by coincidence, but they both seemed pleased by the development.

When everything was finally put in its place, Liv gave Juliette a high five. "Good job! You want to come to Joe's with me? I still owe you dinner."

"I'd love to."

Kane and Laura seemed pleased to have some alone time together, thinking that their girls were just giving them space. Juliette let them think that. It wouldn't do to have Laura thinking that Juliette had undue interest in Liv.

Juliette realized there was something between

her and Liv bubbling below the surface. She had never before questioned her sexuality, but here she was doing just that.

Accepting Liv's sexuality was one things. Accepting that her daughter might not be as straight as she had always appeared would be quite another hurdle for Laura. One that Juliette wasn't sure she would ever recover from.

Anyway, that shouldn't be a problem, because Juliette *was* straight. She had always felt confident in that. She wanted to spend more time with Liv purely from a friendship perspective. It must be the new step-sister thing. Juliette had always wanted a sibling, and to suddenly be given one that she got on so well with, that must be what was triggering Juliette's slightly confused feelings.

It didn't matter how Liv's cleavage somehow seemed suddenly intriguing to Juliette. She promised herself she wouldn't look anywhere except Liv's face the entire evening.

This proved to be... challenging. Why did Liv have to like such tight shirts? Juliette was all for body positivity – and there was a lot for Liv to be positive about when it came to her body – and confidence, but did Liv really have to display that confidence so thoroughly in front of her?

Fuck, she sounded like her mother. Juliette needed to get her head straight, and fast.

You are straight, Juliette.

To distract herself from the enticing sight, she forced herself to stare into Liv's eyes – this hardly helped matters; Juliette had never seen such beautiful eyes before – and start a conversation.

What on earth is happening to me? She is my new sister! Get a grip, Juliette!

"So, it sounds like you love your work. Tell me more about it?"

"It's really amazing. Managing a business is so satisfying – seeing your actions have a direct effect on everything around you. It's a delicate balancing act, keeping employees happy while making sure everyone works to their fullest capacity, but when you get it right, it's amazing. It's everything I ever wanted – to make a success of myself, to make my mother proud."

Juliette was surprised. Most corporate CEOs were obsessed with profit and little else, but Liv hadn't mentioned money at all. Though the business world definitely wasn't for her, the way Liv described it, Juliette could see the appeal.

"I don't know much about Aimee. Laura just said that she died a long time ago."

"Yeah. It was tough. Really, so hard. It still is. I loved her so very much and nothing is the same without her. It took my dad years to get over it. Well, obviously you never get over something like that, but you know what I mean. He needed to move on. He couldn't spend the rest of forever alone and I know she wouldn't have wanted that. I'm so glad he's finally found someone who makes him happy.."

"I'm glad, too. My dad left when I was just two. I guess he decided raising kids wasn't for him."

"Dick. Running out on you was inexcusable. When you decide to have children, you take responsibility for them. You don't just get to leave."

Juliette shrugged. "My mom thinks so, too. She was really angry about it for a long time. I'm glad he left, though. I mean, I would have loved to grow up with a father, but a father who wanted me. Having a father who was only staying resentfully would have really fucked me up."

"I suppose that's true. That's a very mature way to look at it."

Why did she have to blush? Why? Juliette hardly ever blushed, except it seemed around Liv, her face seemed to have the on-off switch of a faulty geyser.

"What about you? Tell me more about your work. Did you always know you wanted to be an artist?"

"Yeah, ever since I was young. My mom always encouraged me, even used my dad's support checks to get my extra art lessons."

"Where do you get your inspiration from? I've seen a lot of art, but nothing like yours."

There her cheeks went, back to flaming again. "I've always seen things like that – as potential to become something beautiful. As I go through life, I'll watch situations and envision how I could capture their essence with paint. That painting I gave you? I got that from swimming in the ocean on a sunny day. It was beautiful out, and I imagined I was a mermaid."

"You certainly captured the beauty of the moment perfectly. Not all of your paintings are about good memories, though."

Juliette was impressed that Liv knew that. Most people didn't understand her art without having it explained to them. "Which ones are you thinking of?"

"Well, the one with the reds and blacks, with all the sharp edges. That's far from peaceful or joyful."

"What do you think it's describing?"

"At a guess, I'd have to say anger."

Juliette nodded. "Anger... and shame. That's why I added those gray streaks."

"What was the situation?"

"My mom wanted to move tables at a restaurant when two guys next to us started kissing. They heard her asking our waiter for somewhere else to sit. I was so pissed, and so embarrassed to be seen with her."

"What did you do?"

Juliette's eyes sought the table. "I... well, I acted rather childishly."

"Now I'm curious."

"I kind of threw my glass of orange juice in her face and told her to fuck off and go sit alone if that's how she felt."

Liv threw her head back and burst out laughing. "Oh, Juliette. I think you and I are going to be good friends."

Juliette laughed as well, now that she knew Liv wasn't going to judge her for her tantrum. "She didn't speak to me for days after that. The guys at the other table, however, invited me to join them. We're good friends now. I bring them over to the house whenever my mom is home. I've told them they don't need to be shy about showing affection toward each other in front of her."

Liv had tears in her eyes from laughter. "Wow, Laura really has a tough time with you, doesn't she?"

"It was a lot worse at first. For a while, she truly believed that she was right about this. I finally got her to realize that her beliefs are wrong, but she still has trouble shaking some of the ingrown bigotry."

"Well, at least she's trying, which is more than I can say for a lot of people. That kind of change doesn't happen overnight."

"I'm really grateful you're giving her a chance. Aside from the homophobia- which I am certainly not excusing- she is mostly a lovely person, very kind and has been a very good mom to me. But, you are doing a big thing. Most people wouldn't be so accepting."

"She makes my dad happy. That's the most important thing."

"But if it came down to a choice, he would be in your corner."

"Yeah, I know. I'm going to make sure it doesn't come down to a choice, though. They're good for each other. I can see how he is around her."

Juliette nodded, her face finally returning to its normal state. "So what kinds of things do you do when you're not working?"

Now, it was Liv's turn to blush. "Um. Not much, really. I don't have much of a life outside of work. I'm pretty much always working."

"Your dad works you hard, huh?"

"No, I can't blame him for the fact that I have no life. He's always begging me to take time off. I just want to do well. I want the company to do well. I want to make my family proud."

"Dedicated. But I suppose I'm not much different – at least in terms of taking time away from work. My work is pretty different to yours, though."

They chatted all through supper. Juliette hardly noticed what she was eating. The more she talked to Liv, the more she liked her.

As hard as she tried to keep her eyes where they belonged, she slipped up several times. Worse, she was sure that Liv noticed.

This was going to be a problem.

This, Liv thought, was going to be a problem.

It wasn't the kind of problem she had envisioned. She had worried that she and Juliette might not get along.

She hadn't considered the possibility that they might get along *too* well. There was something about Juliette that just drew her in. Sure, if Liv had a type, Juliette would be it. Maybe if she didn't look the way she did, things could have been different. They could have just been really close friends, and that would have been the end of it. Juliette was straight anyway, wasn't she?

However, Juliette's appearance complicated

things. Liv had been totally unprepared to face a woman like Juliette. Her blonde messy hair hung just past her shoulders, framing her face perfectly. She was pale with a dusting of adorable little freckles across her nose, and big blue eyes that made her look like an angel. Her lips were full. Full and tempting. Juliette liked to wear lipstick and the red of her lips lived long inside of Liv's mind.

And her body... fuck, it made Liv's mouth dry just to think of it. Juliette was slim, with understated curves and small breasts that would fit perfectly into Liv's hands. She had always been a sucker for small breasts. She wondered what Juliette's nipples were like.

Fuck, Liv. Stop it! She is your new step-sister!

She reminded herself that Juliette was straight. Making a move on her would surely make things weird between them, and that was the last thing either of them needed.

Was Juliette straight, though? Because the looks she had been giving Liv ever since they met were decidedly not straight. Straight women didn't look at other women like that. Liv would know. Like all lesbians, she had experienced the struggle fancying women who simply weren't into women.

She knew how to tell the difference, and Juliette was setting off her gaydar like fireworks on Guy Fawkes Day.

However, that didn't mean it would be a good idea to do something stupid like kiss her. If she was gay, Juliette was clearly repressed, and with the beliefs her mother still somewhat held, Liv didn't blame her.

She would simply have to let Juliette come to that realization in her own time.

But, a small voice in her head argued, how would Juliette ever come to that realization on her own? She had every reason to want to continue thinking she was straight. Maybe all she needed was a little nudge...

Nope. She was so not going there. Things were going fantastically between her and Juliette. So what if Liv wanted her in a way that Juliette didn't return? She was an adult and could deal with unrequited feelings.

At the very least, she knew that Juliette liked her, as a friend if nothing else.

Liv was home early, again. Her dad was delighted that she had taken to coming home at five rather than staying several hours late.

Kane and Laura weren't home yet, which

suited Liv just fine. She dropped her briefcase off in her room and shrugged off her suit jacket before heading straight to Juliette's studio- a side building close to the house, that had been mostly unused before Juliette and Laura had moved in.

Juliette was painting, as usual, her fine delicate hand on the paintbrush, but she looked up when Liv walked in. She was all full lips and big blue eyes and she just oozed sex appeal. She wore a loose fitting tunic in blue that brought out the beautiful color of her eyes.

"Hey, Liv. Take a seat."

They had moved one of the couches from the lounge in here so that Liv could relax and spend time with Juliette. She loved seeing Juliette paint. It was utterly mesmerizing.

"Still not that one, huh?"

"Yeah, it's giving me some trouble."

"It's beautiful."

"You think everything I do is beautiful." Her voice was lyrical and Liv craved more of it.

"Because it is."

"Thanks, but I want it to be more than beautiful. I want it to be perfect."

"You never told me what this one is about."

"What do you think?"

Liv thought about it for a moment. "Well, the rainbow colors remind me of pride."

"That's right. It was inspired by you. I love how you're just so completely you, no matter what anyone else thinks."

Knowing that she was the inspiration for one of Juliette's paintings sent butterflies fluttering through her stomach.

"What else?" There was always more, and Liv was getting better at picking out the more subtle meanings, though she was struggling to tell with this one. Perhaps because it wasn't complete yet.

"Look at these curves here. What do they remind you of?"

"Hm. They look kind of like a woman's body – something about the swells there reminds me of hips, or breasts."

"Very good. You'll see the orange, pink and white I added here, for the lesbian flag."

"I don't understand what more you want from it. It's perfect."

"I want to give it more of a shimmery look – like a translucent layer on the top, to make it look kind of like it's made of glass."

"Why glass?"

"Glass is fragile and beautiful, just like the

peace queer folks enjoy. It is too easily shattered by those who think their love is wrong."

That was so touching, it nearly brought tears to Liv's eyes. She was struck once again by the powerful urge to kiss Juliette. She stood up, drawn to her as though Juliette was a human-sized magnet and she was a hapless iron filing.

"You're so talented," Liv murmured. Her eyes flicked to Juliette's lips without her permission. Desire was quickly outweighing rational thought. She looked back into Juliette's eyes to see that Juliette's gaze was fixed on Liv's lips.

Liv leaned forward.

"Juliette? Liv? Are you in here?"

They jumped apart as though an electric pulse had gone through them. Liv tried not to look too guilty as Laura walked in.

"There you are. Dinner is ready."

Was it dinner time already? Liv glanced at the time to see that she'd been watching Juliette paint for nearly two hours now.

"Great." She cleared her throat, trying to get her voice to sound less squeaky. "We'll be right out."

Juliette looked shaken. Liv wondered whether

she was disappointed or relieved that the almost-kiss had been interrupted.

All through dinner, Liv and Juliette spoke little, both immersed in their own thoughts, letting Laura and Kane carry on the conversation.

When dinner was finished, Liv followed Juliette to her room. This wasn't unusual. They often spent time together talking before bed. This time, though, there was a subtle tension between them.

Liv perched on the edge of Juliette's bed, and Juliette sat beside her. They usually sprawled out on opposite ends of the mattress, but Liv was too anxious to lie down right now.

"So... we were kind of interrupted earlier."

Juliette didn't say anything. Liv knew that this was a bad idea, but she had made her decision. She needed to know if Juliette regretted being stopped before kissing or not, and there was one sure way to find out.

Liv pressed a hand to Juliette's cheek. "Tell me if you want me to stop," she whispered. Very slowly, she leaned in and pressed her lips to Juliette's."

For a moment, Liv thought it was going to go exactly as she hoped. Juliette's eyes fluttered shut and her lips parted slightly... then she leaped up, staggering three steps away from Liv, her eyes wide.

"Stop, Liv! I don't – I'm – this is a mistake. You should go now."

Fuck. Fuck, fuck, fuck, she'd really screwed up this time. Of course, Juliette didn't want her. Juliette had already made it clear she was straight – she had the straight ally flag hanging in her room, for fuck's sake. Liv was the biggest idiot ever to have lived. She had misread Juliette's looks completely, transferring her own desire and fooling herself into believing that her feelings were returned.

"I'm sorry. Shit, I'm so sorry, Juliette. I didn't – I thought you wanted me."

"Liv, I like you a lot – as a friend. Nothing more than that. Please, I can't do this."

"Of course. Forgive me. I should go."

Liv dashed out of the room, fighting back tears. She had kissed a woman who didn't want her, knowing that said woman was straight.

She was the biggest piece of shit alive. How could she be so stupid?

Liv ran to her room, losing the fight against tears. She felt awful. How could she ever make this up to Juliette? How would she look her in the eye? What if Juliette refused to speak to her ever again?

If it came down to it, she knew that Kane would choose her side, and Laura would choose Juliette's. Liv would never be able to live with herself if Kane and Laura split up because of her blunder.

How could she fix this? She desperately wanted to do something about it now, but that would be the opposite of helpful. If she pushed herself on Juliette now, tried to force her to hear her apologies when Juliette clearly wanted to be left alone, she would make things worse rather than better.

No, Liv would have to control herself. Too bad her sudden commitment to self-control was coming too late. Nevertheless, she could at least avoid making this catastrophe any worse than it already was.

Would Juliette tell Laura? Liv wouldn't blame her if she wanted to confide in her mother, but if she did, it would pretty much spell death for Laura and Kane's relationship.

Laura would be furious at Liv, and rightly so. Kane would defend her, and the resulting fight would be relationship-ending.

Surely, Juliette wouldn't tell Laura, though. She was also invested in seeing their parents happy, and she had to realize the consequences as well as Liv did. Liv wanted to go back and try to secure her silence now, but once more, she used her newfound self-control to prevent herself from leaving the room.

She had to think with her head now. Way too late, but better late than never, right?

Liv could only hope that she hadn't ruined everything irreparably.

4

JULIETTE

Juliette had never had a panic attack, but she was fairly certain she was having one now. The walls seemed to be closing in on her and the room was spinning. It was becoming increasingly difficult to draw breath.

Was this a panic attack or a heart attack? Should she be calling an ambulance?

No, this had to be panic. She could feel terror racing through her insides, which it had been from the moment she felt Liv's lips against hers, before she had begun to experience any physical symptoms.

Not terror because she didn't want the kiss, terror because she did want it. She really wanted it, and what that meant just seemed too big to comprehend in the moment.

Juliette had no idea how to deal with a panic attack. She had seen people use paper bags on TV. Surely there must be a paper bag around somewhere.

She pulled open drawers, her hands shaking so badly that she sent socks and panties flying everywhere. One of the drawers came flying out of its place entirely and crashed onto the floor.

Giving up on the paper bag idea, she let her knees give out and crumpled to the floor, trying to breathe evenly.

She wouldn't think about the kiss – that would surely send her spiraling deeper into the panic attack. Juliette put her hands on her stomach and focused on expanding and contracting it, filling her lungs with air and then expelling that air as slowly as she could.

She didn't know how long it took for her breathing to return to normal, but it seemed like forever. When she finally no longer felt like she was suffocating, Juliette let out a soft moan of relief. The bed was too far away, so she lay down on the floor, drawing her knees up to her chest.

What the fuck was that?

She didn't blame Liv for kissing her. Liv had told her to say if she must stop, and Juliette had kept stupidly silent. The moment had felt magical. She had let Liv kiss her, so this entire disaster was entirely her fault.

The problem wasn't that Liv had kissed her. If it had just been that, it would have been easy. Juliette would have politely told Liv that she didn't return her interest, and they could have continued being friends.

Except.

Juliette had enjoyed the kiss.

She wasn't supposed to enjoy a kiss from Liv. She wasn't supposed to enjoy a kiss from *any* woman. She was as straight as they came. She was into men. She had sex with men. She dated men. Surely, that meant she was straight?

Sure, nothing had ever lasted and she had never been that sad about that, but that was just because she hadn't found the right guy yet. Loads of straight women struggled to find guys they were compatible with. Some of her friends had even confided in their struggles. Dating was difficult, not only because you had to find someone you were emotionally compatible with, but someone you were sexually compatible with.

She simply hadn't found someone she was compatible with.

Except Liv.

No, she couldn't be compatible with Liv. What would her mother say if she caught the two of them kissing? Juliette would be disowned and kicked out of the house. She did well enough in her own career that she could afford to support herself financially, but that was hardly the point.

She loved her mother and it would break her heart to lose that love. Laura may learn to accept Liv, but she would never accept homosexuality from her own daughter. Just the thought was laughable.

What was she going to do? How could she look into her mom's eyes, knowing that she was lying to her? Not lying directly, but certainly by omission. If Laura knew that Juliette was having doubts about her own sexuality she'd be horrified.

There was only one thing for it. Juliette would have to prove, once and for all, that she was straight – for her own sake as well as her mother's.

She didn't know if Liv would be willing to help her, after Juliette had so rudely kicked her out. She would have to do some groveling if she was going to earn forgiveness.

Juliette was too upset and shaken to do anything tonight. She wanted to talk to Liv after breakfast the next day, but by the time she was awake, Liv had already left for work. She didn't usually leave this early. Juliette didn't blame Liv for avoiding her, but Liv would have to come home sometime. Juliette would get her chance, sooner or later.

It turned out that later was how it was going to be. For three days, Juliette barely saw Liv. Liv didn't even look at her, let alone speak to her.

Juliette decided to take matters into her own hands. She stopped by Joe's just before Liv's lunch hour was about to start and got takeaways.

Then, drove to Aimee Enterprises' headquarters and marched confidently to the front desk.

"Hi, I'm here to see Olivia Jones."

"Do you have an appointment?"

"No – but I'm her stepsister, Juliette. I brought her lunch."

The secretary eyed her suspiciously. "Please, just tell her I'm here." She hoped Liv would agree to see her. "Tell her I brought her a Joe's cheese-burger." Hopefully that would sweeten the deal.

"Alright, give me a minute." The secretary made a call, and hung up after a short exchange.

"You can go up. Seventeenth floor, second door on the left."

"Thank you."

Nerves flared, creating waves in Juliette's stomach as she made her way to Liv's office. When she knocked, Liv called for her to come in.

Juliette was surprised to see Liv feeling every bit as nervous as she felt. Her face looked tight and drawn and her green eyes looked nervous. She ran a hand through her short wavy hair. "Hi," Juliette said quietly. "Can we talk? Please? I brought food."

"Yes, I suppose we had better talk," Liv sighed. She looked immaculate as usual in a navy blue pant suit. She was smart and effortlessly cool. Liv never wore make up and she didn't need it. Her skin was luminescent. "Please, sit down."

Juliette perched on the edge of one of the chairs opposite the desk. She opened her mouth to speak, but Liv beat her to it.

"Juliette... words can't begin to express how sorry I am. My actions were inexcusable. I know you are straight, and I kissed you anyway. I was absolutely in the wrong. I am honestly ashamed at myself–"

"Liv, stop!" Juliette was genuinely shocked. "You didn't do anything wrong."

"I kissed you when I knew –" Liv's green eyes were wide and full of guilt.

"No. Liv, please, just listen to me. I told you I was straight, but then I gave you every reason to believe otherwise with my actions. It's no wonder you were confused. Besides, you told me to say if I wanted you to stop, remember? I kept my mouth shut, and that's on me. Is this why you've been avoiding me? Because you felt guilty?"

"What else would I feel?"

"Honestly? I thought you'd be angry."

"Angry?"

"Furious. I thought that's why you wouldn't look at me."

"Why in the world would I be angry with you, Juliette?"

"I treated you horribly. I let you kiss me, then I threw you out like it was nothing. It... it wasn't nothing, Liv."

Liv's eyes widened. "It wasn't?"

"No," Juliette admitted. "I... I think I liked it."

"You think?"

"I mean, I'm obviously confused. I really like you as a person, and I was letting my feelings of warmth toward you get mixed up in my body."

"I don't think that's how it works..."

"Of course that's how it works. What else would explain my... reaction?"

"I hate to point out the obvious, but maybe you're not as straight as you thought."

"I've always dated guys. I've never been into women before."

"That doesn't make you straight."

"You're right. That in itself is not a defining factor. I need to sort this out once and for all. I need to prove that I really am straight."

"How in the world would you prove something like that?"

"Well, it is a big ask, and I absolutely imagine you will say no. I want to... experiment with you. See through my feelings for you. Soon enough, I'll realize that I only care about you like a friend, and I only admire your body because you're so beautiful – the same way any straight woman would admire a beautiful woman."

"What if you just end up proving the opposite?"

"I won't. I. Am. Straight. I can't imagine things

would get very far between us." Juliette said through gritted teeth. "Look, Liv, I understand completely if this isn't for you. I've messed you around already. This would be messing you around more. It is super messy anyway because we are step-sisters. But, I know I need to find some kind of way to trial this. I'm sure I can find someone else. That's what dating apps are for. I can –"

"Absolutely not." Liv's face that had looked curious and confused was suddenly resolute. "I am not entrusting you to some stranger to go on this journey with. Of course, I'll help you."

"Really?"

"Yeah, I will. You may turn out not to be into women, but I'm sure it's not escaped your notice that I am super into you. I'd love to date you, even if it's only for a short time."

"Date?" Juliette squeaked. "I was thinking of just... physical experimentation.. like um.. kissing."

"We should do both. I mean, if you want to be thorough. You know that romantic and sexual attraction aren't the same. It could be you're into women physically but not romantically, or vice versa. You want to prove that you're straight on all fronts, right?"

"Right." Juliette hadn't thought of that, but the idea of dating Liv was enticing – all in the name of proving her straightness, of course. "In that case, where do we start?"

"Right here. This is our first official lunch date. Come here, let's sit on the couch."

They moved to the couch, taking their food with them. Liv dug into her burger. It was hilarious how much she loved those burgers. They weren't even that good, but Liv went crazy for them. Juliette felt a fond smile gracing her face as she started in on her chicken wrap.

"So, what made you finally decide to talk to me? It must have been a scary conversation to initiate."

"Yeah, but not knowing for sure is driving me crazy. I couldn't take it anymore. How... how was it for you?"

"Discovering my sexuality, you mean? Pretty boring. I always knew I was into women, from the time I understood what it mean to be into anyone. When I was old enough to have the sex talk, my dad gave me the rundown on gay and straight sex. It's all the same thing to him – all sex, all love. I never even officially came out. I just turned up at the house one day with a girl I liked and told him that we were going on a date."

"How did he react?"

"He was ecstatic. I was a bit of a late bloomer. He was worried that I wouldn't find someone. Of course, like most teenage relationships, it ended after not too long, but I'm still glad it happened. Joanne moved to Europe, but we still keep in contact. She has a wife, now, and she's pregnant with their first child."

Wow. It was incredible to Juliette that things were so easy for some people. For her, it wouldn't be that easy.

But, she reminded herself, it wouldn't come to that. Liv had agreed to help her prove to herself that she was straight. This was going to work.

The finished eating and put their takeaway packets aside. Juliette wondered if Liv would kiss her again, and found she was more excited than nervous about the prospect.

"Come here."

She moved closer to Liv, but instead of kissing her, Liv pulled Juliette so that her head was resting on Liv's lap. Juliette looked up at her as Liv started playing with her hair. "Tell me if you don't like it. We can stop."

"No, I like it." She liked it way, way too much. Not in a sexual way, but in a gooey, stay-with-me-forever kind of way, which was almost worse. She knew she had never felt this comfortable with a guy before.

Juliette let her eyes slip closed as she enjoyed the sensation.

"I think we should take this real slow. This is going to be an emotional journey for you, and I don't want to push you until you're uncomfortable. If I do anything you don't like, you have to agree to let me know immediately, or the deal is off. Agreed?"

"Agreed." Juliette felt like she would agree to anything in this position. Liv's hands were like magic, sending waves of relaxation and contentment through her body and soul.

Too soon, Liv's phone rang. She groaned and answered.

"Olivia Jones. Yes. Alright, thank you. I'll handle it."

She hung up and shot Juliette an apologetic look. "I have to get back to work. Sorry to cut this short."

"No need to apologize – I'm the one who ambushed you at work with no warning."

"So warn me next time. We should do this again."

"Yeah, we should! Second date tomorrow?"

Liv grinned. "Second date tomorrow. Just in the name of proving your heterosexuality. I'll see you at home, Juliette. Oh, and thanks for the burger."

"You are most welcome. See you later."

Juliette practically skipped out of the office building. She shouldn't be this giddy, but she didn't care. She was ecstatic to be speaking terms with Liv, and almost painfully excited about the coming weeks. Sure, it would have end, but she was still delighted to have given herself permission to experiment with Liv.

This had been a great idea. She would ultimately prove to herself she was straight, but for now, she gave herself permission to enjoy this.

5

L iv couldn't believe how lucky she'd gotten. Not only did Juliette not blame her for the kiss, but she had agreed to date.

Though Juliette was sure it would end in her figuring out she was straight, Liv was far from convinced. Sure, straight people did experiment with their sexuality, just like gay people did. So in theory, it was completely possible that Juliette was indeed straight and just curious.

However, Liv didn't think that was the case in this instance. She couldn't pin down what made her so sure it was more than curiosity for Juliette, but she was nonetheless convinced that Juliette was in fact gay.

And what better way to convince her than show her how amazing a relationship with someone she could truly care for and be attracted to could be?

Liv was going to make this good for Juliette. Even if it did end – because even if Juliette was gay, that didn't necessarily mean she and Liv would work out – Liv was determined to make Juliette's first time dating a woman a positive experience for her.

She momentarily thought it might be a bad idea- Juliette being her stepsister and everything, but Liv had always pursued love freely and she didn't intend to change that now.

The next day, she dressed particularly carefully, in one of the tight shirts she knew Juliette liked (even though Juliette had yet to admit it,) and a smart red pantsuit that really showed off her ass. Liv stopped by a florist on the way to work to get some sunflowers – Juliette's favorite flower.

She didn't get much work done that morning.

She was too excited about lunch time. She and Juliette had shared plenty of meals together, but now it was different. Now, they were dating, and those meals took on a whole new meaning. Liv was finally free to feel and do what she wanted, without worrying about upsetting Juliette or ruining things between them.

Juliette knocked ten minutes early. "Sorry, I know I'm early. If you're still busy I can –"

"No, I'm not busy," Liv said quickly. "Please, come in."

They sat down on the couch and Juliette handed her another Joe's burger. "You know, you really should eat something other than burgers. They're not good for you."

"Yeah, but I'd rather die young than live a sad, burger-less life."

"Bah, you can still have them. It's all about moderation. Besides, there's plenty of nice food at Joe's. This wrap, for instance, has half the carbs and fat, but it's still really delicious and –"

Liv burst out laughing. "Look at you, worrying for my health. It's like we're an old married couple already."

She immediately regretted the comment, wondering if it would freak Juliette out. However,

Juliette just laughed too. "If we get married, you are *so* cutting back on the burgers."

She knew that Juliette was just joking around with her, but the words sent a thrill through Liv's veins nonetheless. "If I have to cut back on the burgers, then you have to cut back on your hours. Sometimes I worry that you've accidentally locked yourself in your studio, with as much time as you spend there."

"Ha, like you're one to talk! You work longer hours than I do." Juliette's full red lips in a smile were so seductive as she teased Liv back.

"I can see we're going to have a lot of marital strife."

"Imagine the couples counseling sessions. We'd probably scare the therapist away."

"Nah, I have the perfect line to effectively end any argument."

"Oh yeah? Now I'm curious." Her blue eyes were wide and expansive like the sky.

"We're having a fight. Tell me you can't even look at me right now."

Juliette played along. "I'm so fucking angry with you, Liv! I can't even look at you right now!" She stood up and turned her back, folding her arms and facing resolutely in the other direction.

"Well, why don't you come and sit on my face so that you don't have to look at it?"

Juliette burst out laughing. She flopped back onto the couch with Liv, laughing so hard it brought tears to her eyes. "That's fucking brilliant."

"It works, too."

"You've actually used that?"

"Yeah, and I can tell you, it ends arguments pretty quickly."

"Yeah we are definitely scarring that couples counselor."

"I didn't say we'd do it with them in the room!"

"Come now, where's the fun in that?"

"You're a menace," Liv muttered. "Do you have an exhibitionist streak? Should we be exploring kinks as well? You want me to tie you up and spank you?"

"Ugh, no thanks. That's one thing I'm sure I'm not into. What about you?"

"I'm not so much into it for myself, but one of my exes loved it. I did some stuff for her. It's not as bad as you think. Very intimate."

"I'll take the intimacy without the spanking, thanks."

"Speaking of which... what do you say to another kiss?"

Liv was watching Juliette carefully for any signs of reluctance, but she saw none. Juliette nodded enthusiastically. "Yeah, let's give it a shot."

"You let me know if you want to stop, yeah? Pull away or tap my shoulder or something. Promise me."

"I promise. You've given yourself a complex over something that didn't even happen. You didn't kiss me when I didn't want you to. I swear, I am not going to kiss anyone I don't want to be kissing."

"Ok, then." Liv moved closer on the couch, so that her and Juliette's knees were touching. She put a hand behind Juliette's neck and drew her closer in.

Their lips brushed lightly at first. Liv paused, giving Juliette time to pull away if she didn't like it, but instead of pulling back, Juliette pressed her lips more firmly to Liv's.

Liv kissed her slowly, exploring Juliette's lips with hers, in no hurry to move things on. They were taking this slowly. Her body had other ideas, but Liv remained firmly in control of her impulses. This was about making things good for Juliette, not chasing her own pleasure at the expense of Juliette's comfort.

Juliette returned the kiss, hesitantly at first, but

then with more confidence. Her lips tasted amazing and Liv wanted more. She wound her fingers into Juliette's hair and drew her closer, letting her mouth sip open, waiting to see if Juliette would take the invitation.

Juliette hesitated for only a moment before sliding her tongue into Liv's mouth. Fuck, she tasted amazing. Liv couldn't get enough of it.

Juliette moaned softly, and that sound sent a bolt of desire through Liv's whole body.

They both jumped apart as someone knocked on the door. Liv internally cursed whoever it was and tried to compose herself.

"Come in." It was Meg, Liv's assistant. Liv liked Meg very much, but right now, she wished only that Meg would go away.

"What is it, Meg?"

She must have not done as good a job as she thought at keeping the sharpness out of her voice, because Meg took an automatic step back. "Sorry to disturb you. It's just that I've got Lessi Corporation on the line. They're wanting to negotiate the terms of our contract."

Liv sighed. "I'll be right there. Just give me a minute."

Meg closed the door behind her as she left. Liv

leaned in to give Juliette one more kiss, just a light little peck on the lips. "We'll continue this later, yeah?"

"Definitely. I'll leave you to your work.'

Juliette kissed Liv one last time before leaving, throwing a parting glance over her shoulder.

Liv didn't remember being this turned on by anyone ever before. She desperately wanted to get away into a bathroom – or even a broom closet would work in a pinch – to do something about her throbbing desire. However, work didn't wait for her just because she was horny.

Liv was frantically busy for the rest of the day. It helped her forget her desire for now, but that returned in full force when she came face to face with Juliette once more at home. Liv knew that it would be smarter to wait until after dinner, when they were less likely to be disturbed, but she wasn't sure if she could wait that long.

"Hey."

Juliette looked up from her painting and immediately put her brush down. "Hey. My room?"

The atmosphere between them was heavy and very sexual. Juliette's beautiful face was seductive. Liv couldn't believe how lucky she was. Things might get messy here- sure. But, it was a risk Liv was willing to take. She was crazy about Juliette. Crazy for her stepsister and it would be foolish to try and deny that to herself.

Liv grinned, glad that Juliette was thinking along the same lines as her. "I was waiting for you to ask."

They were kissing the moment the door closed behind them. Liv groaned as Juliette pressed their bodies together, entwining her arms around Liv's waist as Liv caressed her face.

"Been thinking about you all day," Liv murmured.

"Me too. I touched myself, imagining what we'd do tonight."

Fuck. Really? She drives me wild.

"I wanted to. I was cursing everyone at work for keeping me busy."

"We'll just have to make up for it now, then, won't we?"

After that, their lips were too busy to do any talking. They made out passionately, swallowing each other's moans and small whimpers. Liv couldn't resist pressing a thigh between Juliette's legs, putting some pressure over her clit. Liv had plenty of skills to pleasure women with, and she knew it.

Juliette gasped and ground into Liv's leg with increasingly frantic movements. Liv knew she was driving her crazy. She increased the pressure.

"Fuck, I'm gonna come. Oh yes, Liv, yes!" Juliette's voice was a whimper. Liv smiled to herself.

I knew damn well she wasn't that straight. Straight women don't come humping another woman's leg while fully clothed.

Liv clapped a hand over Juliette's mouth to smother her cry as Juliette convulsed on her leg, her arms clutching Liv so tightly that it was hard to tell whose body was whose. Liv felt a surge of wetness spreading over her leg as Juliette came hard, finally going lax in Liv's arms.

Liv felt momentarily very pleased with herself. There was nothing she enjoyed more than a beautiful woman coming apart in her arms.

They barely had time to recover before Laura's voice rudely interrupted their moment. "Girls, it's dinner time!"

Liv groaned in frustration. She was so horny she felt like she might just explode. She was sorely tempted to just lock the door carry on, but she knew that would raise suspicions that Juliette didn't want.

"Later," Juliette promised.

"Yes, please." Liv glanced in the mirror and groaned again. "Look at my eyes! They're going to think I'm high."

Her pupils were blown wide and frantic with need.

"It'll be fine. I doubt they'll even notice. Come on, we do not want them coming up here. We both need a change of clothes."

Juliette blushed as she looked down at the mess she'd made. "I've never done that before."

"I'll take that as a compliment. But you're right – we don't have time to talk right now."

Almost as much as she wanted to come, Liv wished she and Juliette had time to talk through what had just happened. There she was, trying to take it slow, but she had once more allowed her body to override her mind's more sensible thoughts.

Still, Juliette didn't seem freaked out at all. If anything, she was just as enthusiastic as Liv was.

Liv hurried to her room and quickly changed her pants before getting to the dining room just as Laura was about to come and call them again.

"Oh, there you are. Where's Juliette?"

"I think she'll be down in a moment."

There was nothing suspicious in the way Laura was looking at her, which was a relief. Liv felt riddled with guilt. Juliette entered the room a minute later, looking adorably flushed.

It was the longest dinner Liv had ever sat through. She tried to answer her father's questions about work attentively, but her eyes kept being drawn back to Juliette. The moment everyone was done eating, Liv grabbed the empty plates and took them to the kitchen, practically fleeing the room with Juliette right on her heels.

"Bed," Juliette said shortly and Liv enjoyed her authoritative tone. Liv threw herself onto the bed, beckoning for Juliette to join her.

"Need you," Liv muttered. "So bad, Juliette."

"Oh, I know. I could see you squirming all through dinner. I... you'll need to tell me how to do this. I've never done it with a woman before."

"Are you sure you want to?" Liv might just die if she didn't, but she had to check. "We don't need to go this fast. I know we were going to take things slow..."

"Fuck slow. I want you, now."

Oh, thank God.

"Then let's get our clothes off."

They undressed and Liv pulled Juliette in for a kiss. They kissed until Liv thought that she might just die of unrealized desire. When she couldn't take it anymore, she pulled back just enough to speak.

"Touch me. Right here."

She guided Juliette's hand to her clit. Juliette's movements were hesitant at first, but quickly became surer as Liv murmured her encouragement. "Just a little lower... circles, yes circles are good... You can be more firm. Oh *yes*, Juliette. That's so good. Fuck, I'm close."

Liv was so on edge already that it didn't take her long. "Faster. Please, faster."

Juliette's hand flew over her clit, rubbing firmly in circles in a way that made Liv lose her grip on reality.

Liv gritted her teeth together to stop herself from crying out aloud as she came into Juliette's hand. It was so intense that it took her breath away, literally. She was actually seeing stars by the time her body allowed her to draw in a desperate gasp of oxygen.

Fuck, why does this particular woman drive me so crazy?!

She pushed Juliette's hand away weakly when the overstimulation became too much.

"Was that good?" Juliette asked anxiously.

"Fuck it, Juliette. That was the best I've ever had."

"You're just saying that to make me feel better."

"I am absolutely not. I wouldn't lie to you, Juliette."

"Really?"

"Really. You do something to me. Something powerful. Now, you look like you could use something to take the edge off, am I right?"

Juliette blushed. "It's so hot watching you come."

"How do you feel about oral?"

"Well, I've had guys do it to me before and I've never really enjoyed it... but maybe it'll be different with you."

"Then come here and sit on my face." Liv knew it was asking a lot for her first time with a woman, but she enjoyed testing Juliette and it was the one thing she herself had not been able to stop thinking about and fantasizing over.

Juliette hesitated a couple of seconds before she began to obey. She carefully arranged herself straddled kneeling over Liv's face, hovering a few inches above her tongue.

"You can get off any time you decide you don't like it," Liv reminded her, desperate to bury herself in Juliette's pussy. She could see how wet Juliette was above her. She could smell the sweet scent of Juliette's arousal and it was driving her crazy.

"Yeah. Ok. Let's do this."

Juliette sounded nervous, but all traces of nerves left her movements when Liv's tongue first flitted over her clit.

"Oh! Oh yes, that's good. Mmm, that's really good."

Juliette began to move on Liv's tongue, taking control of the experience. Liv let her do what she wanted. She had plenty of experience in this and knew how to make it good for Juliette. Liv put her all into licking Juliette into a frenzy.

Juliette was making tiny whimpers under her breath, clearly enjoying the experience a lot.

Straight? I don't fucking think so.

Liv smiled to herself as she gripped Juliette's thighs tighter and pulled Juliette down onto her face more, knowing the increased pressure would take Juliette closer.

"Liv, I'm –"

She wasn't able to give any more warning than that. Juliette ground herself so hard onto Liv's tongue that Liv had to hold her breath as Juliette came hard and wet into her mouth. Liv swallowed fast and smiled to herself.

Fuck, yes.

Juliette sighed as she finally pulled a leg over Liv's face, allowing Liv to breathe finally. Although if she had suffocated with Juliette sitting on her face, she knew she would have died happy. Juliette flopped down next to Liv on the bed, but Liv wasn't having that. She immediately pulled Liv into her arms, spooning her and resting her hands on Juliette's stomach.

"This is nice," Juliette mumbled.

Juliette is super gay. Even more than I had first thought.

"Yeah."

They lay in silence for a while. Liv was so blissed out that it took a few moments for her to realize that Juliette was shaking.

"Juliette?" She propped herself up on one elbow and was horrified to see that Juliette had tears streaming from her eyes.

"Juliette? What's wrong?"

Liv panicked. She'd done something wrong.

Juliette hadn't really enjoyed it, or perhaps it was simply that they were moving too fast. She knew that she shouldn't have let her body get ahead of her brain *again*. She'd fucked things up royally, and once more, Juliette was the one to pay the price.

"I – I –"

"It's ok if you didn't like it," Liv soothed. "There's no pressure, Juliette."

"No, that's not it – it's that I *did* like it. A lot."

Oh. Liv could only imagine how confusing this must be for Juliette. She had been so busy proving Juliette was gay, she had forgotten to think about what it might be like for Juliette going through that discovery. "That's fine, too," she assured her. "We're just experimenting, remember? There are bound to be things you like and don't like. So, we put oral sex on the list of things you like. A lot."

"That's just it – I shouldn't be liking any of this with a woman, let alone liking it way more than I ever did with a man. Liv... I think I might be a little bit gay."

VERY VERY GAY.

Liv felt a small smile creep over her face.

"That's ok, Juliette. I swear, there's nothing wrong with it."

"I know that! You know I do. I just... I can't be gay."

"Why not?"

"You know my mother. She'd never accept me."

"She'll come around. If anything, you coming out will help speed up her journey."

"No!" Juliette gasped. "Liv, I can't come out. You mustn't say anything to her – promise me!"

"Shh, it's ok. I promise. I'm not going to out you, Juliette. You can come out in your own time."

"I can't. This has to stay a secret."

Liv knew that coming out was a big deal to many people, and the last thing she wanted to do was pressure Juliette. She was sure that Juliette would navigate her own coming out journey eventually, but right now, she needed to support Juliette's current decision.

"Whatever you decide is ok. You are in control, Juliette."

"It doesn't feel like it. It feels like my life is spinning out of my control. I don't want to be gay, Liv."

"Well, you know what I think – that you should live your life as who you are. But you don't have to take my advice. No one is forcing you to date or sleep with women if you don't want to. You are in control of who you spend time with and what you do with them. You are in control of whether or not you come out. I promise, even though it feels like it's all falling apart, it's really not. I'm here for you, whatever happens."

Juliette sighed as she turned and nestled her head into Liv's breasts. It felt good. "Yeah, I guess you're right. It just feels overwhelming right now."

"Of course it does. You've spent your whole life thinking you're straight and now you're having some serious doubts like that. It's a real turnabout on your own axis. Just give it time. You'll come around to the idea."

"I hope so. It's not me I'm worried about, though."

"The only person who is going to tell your mom about this is you, and if you decide to do that, it'll only be when you're good and ready. Maybe you could even wait until she has kicked the last of her unsavory beliefs before doing it."

"Is this it, then? Am I definitely gay?"

Yes. The way you came for me. The way fucking me turned you on. Definitely.

"That's not a question I can answer for you, but the fact that you enjoyed this so much when you said you never really enjoyed it with men is a strong indicator that you probably aren't so straight. Do you feel like you're attracted to men at all?"

"I thought I was, but now I'm having doubts. I mean, I can tell when a man is logically attractive, but that doesn't make me want to do anything with him. It's not like with you. All I want is to get my hands all over you. I've never felt like that about a guy before."

Yeah, she was definitely gay. However, Liv didn't want to freak her out, so she kept that thought to herself. "We can keep experimenting. Once is hardly grounds to make a final decision."

And ok, there was some selfishness to her statement. She was enjoying this. No, that wasn't putting it strongly enough. Liv was loving this, more than she'd ever loved anything in her life. She didn't want her dates and sexual encounters with Juliette to end. She wanted to draw it out for as long as possible, until she had convinced Juliette that the 'experiment' didn't have to end at all.

"You're right. I could still turn out to be straight," Juliette added hopefully.

"Honestly, I wouldn't count on it. But, it isn't as simple as straight or gay. There are a lot of people who are somewhere in between. And, you never know what might happen. We can just keep going at your pace – even slow down if you want."

"I don't want that," Juliette said quickly. "I want more of this. I want all of this. With you."

"Then we're on the same page."

Fucking my 'straight' stepsister. Great work, Liv!

They lay together for a while longer. Liv was relieved that Juliette had at least stopped crying, though her expression was still troubled.

"I should go." Liv reluctantly disentangled herself from Juliette's arms. "If you want to keep this secret from your mother, it won't do to have her walking in on us naked in bed together."

Juliette chuckled weakly. "Yeah, I somehow don't think we'd manage to explain that away. It is a good job my bedroom is pretty separate from the rest of the house. Goodnight, Liv."

"Goodnight, Juliette."

Liv was still on cloud nine as she drifted to her bedroom.

When she and Juliette started this, she hadn't been sure where it would go, but so far, it was going better than she had ever dreamed.

Messy? Sure. But, that didn't phase Liv.

She couldn't wait for what came next.

"You two going out again?" Laura was eyeing them beadily, and Juliette felt a familiar flash of fear. Did her mother suspect anything? She and Liv had been going on a lot of dates together recently, but Laura had no reason to suspect they were dates. As far as she knew, Liv and Juliette were just good friends.

"Yeah, we were thinking of going to Joe's," Liv said lightly.

They weren't going to Joe's. They had reservations at a romantic, fancy restaurant, but Laura wasn't to know that. Juliette knew that Liv was uncomfortable with lying, and appreciated that Liv did it anyway for her sake.

"Ok, well enjoy yourselves. Juliette, can I have a word before you go?"

"Sure." Juliette told herself not to freak out. It was probably nothing.

She followed her mom through to the living room. "What's up?"

"Juliette, you need to be careful around Liv."

Julitte's heart sank. "What are you talking about?"

"I see the way she looks at you. I think she wants you in a more... unsavory manner than just friendship."

"Mom!" Juliette tried to hide her fear behind the indignant outburst that would have happened anyway at those words, even if she and Liv had been just friends. "Even if Liv did want me in that way, it wouldn't be unsavory! Stop being a bigot."

"But she looks at you like –"

"I don't care how you think she looks at me. Liv and I are just friends. That's it. But if she did like me as more than a friend, that would be ok. I would politely let her know that I didn't return the interest and we'd continue as friends. Ok?"

"Yeah. Ok." Her mom at least seemed reassured by this. Juliette couldn't help wonder if she had been noticing the way she looked at Liv. If she noticed the way Liv was looking at her, it only made sense that she would see the looks going in the other direction.

They were going to have to be more careful, but Juliette wasn't sure how. She couldn't exactly avoid looking at Liv, and she had no idea how to modify what her eyes held to the view of another.

Liv was waiting for her at the door. They had their smart evening wear carefully packed into Liv's car. They could hardly leave the house like that while pretending they were going to Joe's.

Liv drove them to the local mall first, where they used the bathroom to get changed. Juliette reflected sadly that some people would find all the cloak-and-dagger exciting, but she just found it exhausting.

Liv was wearing some tight navy blue pants that made her ass look incredible and a low cut silk shirt that clung to her body. As usual, Liv was effortlessly cool and effortlessly sexy.

Fuck, she is so beautiful. And sexy. Fuck.

Liv seemed to be in good spirits, though, and that lifted Juliette's mood, too. She was looking forward to tonight. They had been on a number of dates by now, but this was the first one that was overtly romantic and couldn't be mistaken at all for two friends hanging out.

When they got to the restaurant, a waiter was ready for them, leading them to a table with a long candle in the middle and an elegant, dark blue table cloth hanging almost to the floor.

Juliette glanced around as she sat down, sure that she would be treated to judgmental looks on every side, but no one paid more than passing attention to them. Two women clearly on a date... and no one cared.

"What are you looking so concerned about?"

"I just – well, I'm expecting someone to confront us, to be honest. My mom certainly would. At least, she would have a year ago. I'm not sure now, but she'd be thinking disapproving thoughts to be sure."

"No one is going to confront us. People nowadays are a lot more accepting than you'd think – and those who aren't know better than to cause a scene in here. Allowing homophobia in your establishment is a sure way to get the worst press possible. They would be kicked out for sure."

That was a comforting thought, because Liv was right. Juliette knew that the manager wouldn't want to risk their restaurant's reputation. She turned her eyes to the menu, which looked absolutely delicious.

They ordered, and while they were waiting for the food to arrive, Liv took Juliette's hand over the table. This time, Juliette didn't bother to look around. She was too focused on the pleasant feeling of Liv's warm hand around hers to think of much else.

"You know, there's a garden out back. I was thinking that after dessert, we could go out and watch the stars together."

Juliette squeezed Liv's hand. "That sounds wonderful."

The date was absolutely perfect. The food was divine, the staff pleasant, and the garden around the back was beautiful. Liv and Juliette sat on a bench. It was chilly, and Liv put an arm around Juliette's shoulders, drawing her in closer as they gazed up at the sky.

Juliette, if she was honest with herself, which she was desperately trying to avoid, knew she was on some level falling in love with Liv.

Liv made her happy in a way that nobody ever had.

"I always liked looking at the stars, you know. A

lot of my paintings are inspired by the feelings they evoke."

"Like what?" Liv asked curiously.

"The feeling of being a tiny speck in the universe – but not in a bad way. Just a small part of something much bigger. It reminds me of who God is and how amazing He was to have created all this."

"That must be a nice feeling."

Juliette knew that Liv wasn't religious, and she'd never felt the need to try to convert her. She knew that some people were all about converting others, but Juliette held the unpopular belief that those who didn't worship as she did weren't destined for hell.

It drove her mother almost as crazy as her pro-LGBTQ+ beliefs did. Laura had tried unsuccessfully to convert both Kane and Liv. Kane had been patient with her, but Liv had just laughed in her face, telling her there was no way. Juliette smiled as she remembered her mother's indignation.

"Yeah, it is. Do you believe in anything? I know you don't believe in God, but is there anything else that guides you?"

"I suppose my own moral compass guides me. Most of my beliefs are the same as the ones my dad taught me growing up, but I've examined them and taken and added what I felt was necessary."

"How do you decide which beliefs are right and which ones aren't?" Juliette had it easy. Everything was written down in a book for her – though to be fair, there were many parts of the book she didn't take literally, or prioritized over others, such as Jesus' command to love your neighbor over some aspects of Leviticus.

"I guess the ones that make me feel proud of my actions are good one, and the ones that cause me to be ashamed are bad ones."

It seemed like a faulty system to Juliette, because how could you trust that your own feelings were correct? However, Liv's beliefs were much the same as hers, and she hadn't found a single objectional thing about Liv's views, so perhaps the system wasn't as faulty as it seemed.

"That makes sense. Ugh, look at the time. We should probably go. Any later and my mom isn't going to buy that we were at Joe's this whole time."

Liv sighed. "Yeah, let's head out."

Juliette was quiet on the drive back, immersed in her thoughts. The date had been enlightening as well as delightful. She knew that she liked dating Liv – she'd known that for a long time.

Tonight, though, was the first night it had hit her just how much she didn't want this to end.

They returned and said hurried goodnights to Laura and Kane before going to Juliette's room, as was their habit in the evenings.

"Liv, I need to talk to you."

Liv stiffened.

"Nothing bad, I promise," Juliette assured her. Liv only seemed to relax a fraction, and Juliette hurried to say what she needed to, sure it would be well-received.

"I don't think we should continue this as an experiment."

Disappointment filled Liv's face. "You want to stop?"

"Absolutely not. What I'm saying is that I don't' want this to be an experiment anymore. I want to date you for real, not just to try things out. I'm gay, Liv, and... and I'm falling in love with you."

Liv's lips were suddenly on hers, hot and passionate. "I feel the same for you," Liv murmured between kisses. "We're going to be great together, Juliette, you'll see."

"We already are."

All thoughts of talking ended as they started stripping each other's clothes off between kisses.

It was a good thing Liv was more observant than Juliette, because Juliette didn't notice anything until Liv was jerking away from her and diving for her clothes.

Then Juliette heard the sound of approaching footsteps. It didn't matter whether it was her mom or Liv's dad. Kane wouldn't take issue, but he also wouldn't lie to his fiancé about it. If they were caught like this, they were doomed.

Juliette frantically shoved her arm through the sleeve of her top, trying to straighten it before the door opened.

There was a knock. "Girls, are you still in there?"

"Just a minute!" Juliette called out frantically, trying to zip up her pants.

The door opened and Laura stuck her head in. Juliette hastily pulled her shirt down to hide the fact that her pants were unzipped. She glanced at Liv, who seemed to have done a better job at getting dressed speedily, though her clothes were still a bit rumpled from lying in a pile on the floor.

"What are you two still doing up? Have you seen the time?"

Juliette didn't know what the time was, but she was sure it was late.

Liv made a show of looking at her watch. "Shoot! I guess we got so caught up in talking that we forgot all about it. You must tell me more tomorrow about the inspiration for that painting, Juliette."

"Of course. I'm always happy to talk about my work."

Laura was eyeing the two of them suspiciously, but she seemed to accept their story, for now. "Well, goodnight, then."

"Goodnight," Juliette and Liv chorused.

"I think she knows," Juliette whispered after the door was closed.

"She can't know. She can only suspect, and as long as we don't give her any solid proof, those suspicions mean nothing. You really should install a lock on that door, though."

"And tell her what? That will just make her more suspicious."

"I suppose. I was thinking, if worst comes to worst, we could pretend I'm posing nude for a painting you're doing."

"And what would we say about the reason for me being naked too?"

"I felt self-conscious to do it alone, so you agreed to do it in solidarity?"

"Weak, Liv."

"Well do you have a better idea?"

"Um. Spilled paint on my clothes?"

"Yeah, because you don't have other clothes to get changed into."

Juliette chuckled along with her. "I guess we'll need to work on our story. But best not to get caught in that position in the first place."

"Agreed. Anyway, I should go, before she comes to check in on us again."

Juliette couldn't help but pull Liv in for one more kiss. "Goodnight, Liv. Sleep well."

"Sleep well, Juliette. I'll see you tomorrow."

The words were a seduction and a promise all rolled into one. When Liv left, Juliette threw herself onto the bed, a silly grin spreading across her face.

She and Liv were dating. For real, not just as an experiment.

If she was being honest with herself, it had been more than an experiment to Juliette for some time now, but it still felt good to make it official.

Her smile faded as she thought about all this meant. It meant that the sneaking around and hiding from their parents would no longer be temporary. That would be the rest of their lives. Did they really want to live like that?

It was worth it, Juliette decided. For Liv, it was worth it. Even if they could never be together openly, they knew what was in their hearts, and that's what mattered, not what other people saw.

Juliette had a brief glimpse of a future she could never have – one where her mother walked her down the aisle and handed her over into Liv's arms... but it wasn't to be. Juliette had better get those ideas out of her head right now, before they threatened to consume her with sadness.

Sad was the last thing she was feeling right now. She was positively elated that Liv had agreed to be with her properly, despite knowing that it would mean a lifetime of lies and hiding. It meant the world to Juliette that Liv valued her that much.

She fell asleep with a smile on her face.

"**O**h, hi!"

"What are you looking at your phone so intently about? Did we get any updates from Lessi Corporation?"

"No, I was just texting Juliette." Texting her dirty messages that were making Liv hot and flustered in all the best ways.

"You two certainly seem to be getting on well." Kane gave her a knowing look that Liv didn't like at all.

"She's become a good friend," Liv said guardedly. She wished more than anything that she could be honest with her father. She was sure that he would be supportive. However, she was also sure that he wouldn't keep it from Laura.

If it was up to her, she and Juliette would brave Laura's reaction, but Liv would never do something like that without clearing it with Juliette first. It had been three months now since they had started dating officially, beyond the guise of 'experiment'. Maybe it was time to broach the subject.

"Did you need anything, Dad?"

"No, I was just checking on you. You seem... distracted."

Liv's insides squirmed guiltily. She had thought she was doing a good job at concentrating on work even when all she wanted to do was spend time with Juliette, but maybe she wasn't doing as well as she'd thought.

"I'm sorry, Dad. I'm just... stressed."

"I told you that you'll work yourself into a nervous breakdown. You should take a week off."

"I can't do that! There's too much work to be done."

"You forget that I was CEO before you. Take a break, Liv. I can hold down the fort for a week."

"Are you sure?"

"Absolutely. Go home. Surprise Juliette." He

winked at her. Fuck, he knew. He may not be saying it, but he knew anyway.

"I'm sure she's busy working," Liv said quickly. "I won't bother her."

"As you like. I'll just be glad to see you having some well-deserved rest."

"Fine, I'll go, but only because you're making me."

"I'll happily take the blame if things fall apart when you're not here – which they won't. Give me a bit of credit here."

Liv chuckled. "Alright, I'm going. Thanks, Dad."

On the way home, she stopped by the florist for some more sunflowers. It was time to have the conversation.

"Liv!" Juliette exclaimed in delight. "You're home early."

"Yeah... my dad convinced me to take some time off."

"That's excellent. Do you want to do lunch? I have some water boiling for pasta."

"Pasta sounds delicious. I got these for you."

Juliette kissed Liv on the cheek as she took the flowers. "Thank you, they're beautiful. Let me just go put these in water."

Liv followed her through to the living room and perched on the edge of the couch. "Juliette, come sit for a moment."

Juliette happily crawled into Liv's lap. "I'm glad you're home."

"Me too. Juliette... please don't freak out, now... but I think my dad knows."

Juliette stiffened. "Knows? About *us?*"

"Don't worry, he's not going to rat us out."

"Did you say something to him?"

"Of course not! You know I'd never do that."

"Then how do you know?"

"I suppose I don't know for sure, but judging by his behavior, he at the very least strongly suspects. But we're ok, I promise. If we had told him outright, he'd be obligated to tell Laura, but I know how his brain works. Given that he has no actual proof, he won't see the point in confiding his possibly wrong suspicious to Laura and just causing a lot of trouble for everyone."

"Are you sure?" Juliette sounded positively panicked and Liv tightened her arms around her, stroking her hair soothingly. "I'm sure. If he was going to say something to her, he would have done it already. We're fine, I promise."

"Ok." Juliette pulled in a deep breath. "Yeah,

ok. You know him better than I do. If you say we're fine, then I believe you."

"You know... it doesn't have to be like this."

"Of course it does. What other option is there?"

"You could come out to your mom."

"You know that's not an option."

"Actually, it is. Sweetheart, I know you find it scary, but you don't have to be scared. I'll be right here with you. It'll be ok, I promise."

"You can't promise something like that, Liv! It won't be ok and you know it!"

Liv was trying to remain patient, but Juliette's closed-mindedness wasn't making it easy. "I truly believe that your mom will accept you with time, but even if she doesn't, it's better to have her know the truth than believe a lie, regardless of whether that means she's in your life or not."

"Easy for you to say! Your dad accepts you – you've never had to make a decision like this!"

"There's no reason to shout, Juliette. We can discuss this calmly."

"There's nothing to discuss!"

"Well I say there is! You're not the only one in this relationship, you know! You think I want to sneak around and hide forever?"

"You knew exactly what you were signing up

from the beginning! Now you choose to complain about it? Don't act like you're the victim here, Liv. I was clear with you from the start. I am not coming out. Ever."

"That's totally unreasonable!"

"Well that's my decision, take it or leave it."

Liv was so angry she was shaking. How could that be Juliette's stance? Did she really expect Liv to lie for the rest of her life? What kind of stupid expectation was that? How could you ask that of someone you cared for?

"You know what? Forget lunch. I'm not hungry anymore. I'm going for a walk."

Liv stormed out of the house, grabbing her jacket on the way out.

She walked quickly, putting all of her rage into her strides. How could Juliette be so inconsiderate? Did she not care about Liv's feelings at all? She knew how much Liv hated lying. Liv had been extremely patient with her, but her patience was running out.

She sighed as she rounded a corner. It was their first fight, not something Liv had been looking forward. She knew it was inevitable – all couples fought, after all – but knowing it was coming didn't make it hurt any less.

Well, there wasn't much Liv could do about the situation. She could either break up with Juliette, or she could accept her decision. Surely, that decision wasn't as final as Juliette thought it was now. Juliette was an honest person, and Liv knew that she didn't like lying either.

Juliette had to come around, sooner or later. Liv just had to dig deep down and find some more patience.

She turned around, heading back toward the house.

Unsurprisingly, Juliette was in her studio. "Knock, knock. Can I come in?"

Juliette sighed and put down her paintbrush. "Yes, please do. Liv... I'm sorry I shouted at you. I stand by my decision, but I handled that conversation badly."

"I know, but I did as well. Coming out is your decision, and you're right that you were clear with me from the start. I shouldn't have allowed myself to get all emotional about it."

Liv didn't expand on her hopes that Juliette would come out sometime in the future. That was sure to start the argument all over again.

"I'll forgive you if you forgive me?" Liv bargained.

"Done." Juliette stepped in for a kiss. "Care to stay? I'm struggling a bit here and I could use my personal muse."

"Well, who am I to stand in the way of an artist's creativity? Of course, I'll stay."

Juliette pushed her current painting away, eyeing Liv speculatively. "You know, I was thinking about that conversation we had a few months back – about what to do if we were caught naked together."

Liv didn't remember that particular conversation, but she liked where Juliette's mind was at.

"Our parents won't be back for a while. I was thinking you could get naked..."

Yeah, Liv definitely liked where this was going.

"... and let me paint you."

Oh. That was not what she'd expected, but certainly not an unwelcome development.

"You want to paint me?"

"Of course. It's been something in my head for a while. If you're up for it, that is."

"I am definitely up for it. Where do you want me? I'm yours to command."

"Well, ideally we'd do it outside, but I somehow don't think that would go down very well with passersby. But I can make it work with you on the sofa. If you could undress and lie down…"

Liv did as Juliette asked, and lay down on the couch. She couldn't resist running a hand down Juliette's hip as she stepped close.

"Hey, no touching! You're going to distract me."

"Mmm, maybe that's not such a bad idea. We haven't done it on this couch yet."

Juliette hesitated, clearly torn. "After," she decided. "We'll make sure to stop before our parents are due home."

"As you wish. In that case, I am putty in your capable hands."

Liv let Juliette position her lying down on the couch, draping her hair artfully around her face and asking her to point her toes a little.

"Ok, perfect. Just hold that position for… I don't know, several hours. To start with."

Lying still for several hours was harder than Liv would have imagined. After three hours, her toes were starting to cramp, but Juliette's face was so intense and happy that Liv didn't want to ruin the moment for her.

The painting was facing sideways, so that Juliette could look at it and glance to the side to see Liv, which meant Liv couldn't see it, but she was sure it would be spectacular. All of Juliette's work was.

When the sun started to set, Juliette finally put her paint brush down.

"Done?"

"No, but we're out of time."

"Do I get to see it?"

"It's far from finished," Juliette hedged. "And I hadn't done this style of painting in years..."

"Come on, Juliette, it's me. I won't laugh if it's awful, I promise." Liv was sure it would be far from awful, but her words seemed to reassure Juliette, who turned the painting to face her.

Liv gasped as she stared into her own face, as lifelike as if she was looking as a photograph. Juliette had taken some artistic license, making her look like she was gracing the airbrushed pages of a fashion magazine.

"This is really how you see me?" Liv murmured.

"You're the most beautiful thing in my world." Juliette carefully put the painting down to dry, facing the wall – probably a good idea. If Laura saw it, it would be disastrous.

The moment Juliette was done, Liv moved to

kiss her, but Juliette danced back. "Put your clothes on first."

"Why?"

"Because I'm going to enjoy stripping them off you – and kissing every inch of you as you're exposed."

Well, Liv could hardly argue with that. She got dressed and stepped eagerly into Juliette's arms. They kissed deeply, both of them affected by the intimacy of what they had been doing all afternoon.

Liv was so into the kiss that she made the fatal flaw of not listening out for footsteps. Juliette sucked at tuning into background noises when she was focused on something, which left it up to Liv... and Liv failed.

"Girls, it's time for – *what are you doing?*"

Liv barely had time to register horror at Laura's voice before Juliette's hands were on her chest, shoving her away so hard she stumbled.

"What the fuck, Liv! How dare you do something like that? You're disgusting!"

Liv stared dumbly at Juliette.

"Get out of my studio. I don't even want to look at you right now."

"Juliette..." It wasn't that Liv didn't understand

what Juliette was doing. What she didn't understand was how Juliette could do it to her.

"You know what? Stay here. I'm leaving."

Juliette stuck her nose in the air and stalked
out. Liv caught a look of satisfaction on Laura's face
before she threw a scornful look in Liv's direction
and followed her daughter out of the room.

Liv was rooted to the spot by shock. Juliette had
shoved her. She'd called her disgusting, all in the
name of keeping up a stupid lie.

Liv couldn't believe it. She knew that Juliette
didn't want to come out, but she had never thought
Juliette would treat her that way, regardless of the
outcome.

Juliette was one of the kindest, most caring,
brilliant people Liv knew... and Juliette had
betrayed her.

She had been deluding herself before. Juliette
was never going to come out. If she would rather
treat Liv like a piece of shit than tell the truth,
clearly the truth wasn't that important to her... or
Liv wasn't. Either way, she and Juliette were over.

Liv didn't go to the kitchen for dinner. She
went to her room, pulled a pillow over her head
and cried until there were no tears left.

The guilt was eating her alive. Juliette couldn't believe what she had done in a moment of panic. What the hell was wrong with her? How could she do that to Liv?

She didn't know how else she could have gotten out of that situation, but there had to have been a better way. If Juliette were less of a shitty person, she would have found that way.

Her guilt intensified when Liv didn't come down for dinner.

"Where's Liv?" Kane glanced at Juliette. "Did she go out for dinner?"

"Um. No, she's here."

"Liv said she got hungry and ate earlier. She's

getting an early night." The lie rolled smoothly off Laura's tongue, and Kane didn't question her. Juliette hated that she was just as good a liar as her mother was. What kind of skill was that to foster?

"She deserves a rest."

She deserved everything, and Juliette couldn't give it to her. Someone like Liv deserved better than to have to live in secret, and Juliette was selfish for trying to make Liv settle for her.

She picked at her food for about ten minutes before giving up and taking her plate away. "I'm also tired. I think I'll get an early night. Goodnight."

"Goodnight, Juliette."

"Sleep well."

Juliette went hesitantly to Liv's room. As she stood outside the door, she heard the muffled sounds of crying. A wave of self-loathing nearly took her off her feet.

Juliette raised a hand and knocked on the door. There was no answer. She didn't know if Liv had even heard her.

Coward that she was, Juliette decided to give Liv some space for tonight. No point in trying to talk to her when she was distraught. She would try again tomorrow.

The truth was, she couldn't bear to see Liv's distress, knowing that she was the cause of it and could do nothing to comfort her. But Juliette hid behind her excuse of waiting for Liv to be calmer before apologizing. It was a good one, and she could almost convince herself that was the reason she retreated to her bedroom. Almost.

Juliette barely slept that night, and when she did, her rest was disturbed by nightmares. She didn't remember them fully when she woke, but she remembered Liv's shattered, horrified face and the pain that flooded her lovely green eyes as Juliette screamed at her.

She went down to breakfast, and wasn't entirely surprised to find that Liv wasn't there.

"Is Liv out?"

"She went to work." Kane frowned in disapproval.

"I thought she had decided to take some time off?" Not that Juliette should be surprised.

"Yes, she had. Funny how she changed her mind." Kane gave Juliette a dark look, which sent shivers down her spine. Liv had been right. Kane knew. However, Laura wasn't looking at Juliette any differently to how she usually did, which clearly meant Kane had kept his mouth shut.

Juliette only wished that yesterday, she'd had the balls to do the same. Instead, she'd screamed at Liv, betrayed her love and broken her heart.

Though he might not know for sure, he clearly suspected that something had happened between them, and that Juliette was to blame for it. If that was the case, he was absolutely correct. Juliette had to work to contain the impulse to break down in tears and beg his forgiveness for what she'd done to his daughter.

She managed to hold herself together through breakfast, and tried to spend the morning painting, but got very little done, having to scrap three canvases before deciding to give it up for the day. When lunchtime came, Juliette went to Joe's and got Liv's usual cheeseburger. She was too queasy with nerves to eat, and got nothing for herself.

She waved at reception as she walked into the building. They all knew her by now, knew that she often spent lunch with Liv, and didn't think anything of her coming and going.

That's why she was surprised when Harold, one of the security guards, stepped in front of her, holding out a hand in a stop motion. "Ms. Montgomery. May I ask where you're going?"

She came to a halt. "To see Liv."

"I'm afraid Ms. Jones doesn't want to see you."

"What? She told you that?"

Though Juliette certainly didn't blame Liv for not wanting to see her, she hadn't expected to be physically barred from her office.

"She did. Now, unless you have other business here, I think it's best that you leave."

"But... but I brought her lunch."

Harold held out his hand for the bag with the burger in it. "I'll see to it that she gets it."

"Um. Ok. Thank you."

Juliette handed over the burger and turned for the door, fighting not to let the tears in her eyes fall.

She was glad that she was the only one who worked from home, which meant she had the entire house to mope in when she got back. She would need to find some way to talk to Liv. She may have ruined everything irreparably, but that didn't mean she wasn't at least going to try to fix things.

Juliette couldn't bear to lose Liv. She didn't want to go through life without Liv at her side. She *needed* to fix this. She was in love with Liv, and she couldn't let the love of her life go.

Yes, she had fucked up badly, but she knew

that Liv loved her too. Surely, Liv would give her a second chance? It would take some time to earn her trust back, but Juliette could deal with that.

Liv came to dinner that night, but she didn't so much as look at Juliette. That was fine. Liv couldn't avoid her forever. They lived in the same house, after all.

Both Kane and Laura were eyeing them warily during the meal. Kane knew what was going on, but Laura didn't.

"Is everything ok with you girls?" she asked hesitantly.

Juliette braced herself. She couldn't expect Liv to lie for her anymore. She knew that Liv wouldn't out her, but she fully expected Liv to tell Laura that no, everything wasn't ok, and how in the world was Juliette supposed to explain that?

Liv didn't react at all like Juliette expected. She pulled on a smile so genuine that even Juliette had trouble telling it was fake. "Of course. I think I'm just tired. I don't have energy for socializing right now. I'm going to get an early night. Sleep well, everyone."

Juliette stared after Liv as she left, dumbstruck.

Liv was *still* lying to protect her, even after what Juliette had done.

What had Juliette ever done to get someone like Liv? Clearly, she didn't deserve her, and Liv had finally figured that out.

Well, Juliette wasn't giving up, at least not yet. If Liv truly didn't want her, then she could say so. Juliette was no stalker, and wouldn't try to harass Liv into being with her if Liv didn't want to, but she certainly wasn't giving up until she knew for sure that all hope was lost.

She knocked on Liv's door. Once more, there was no answer.

Well this time, she wasn't giving up so easily. Juliette opened the door and stepped inside, closing it softly behind her.

"Hi, Liv."

"Can you not take a hint, Juliette?" Liv snapped. "I don't want to talk to you."

"You don't need to talk. I'll be the one doing the talking."

Liv folded her arms and glared at the spot of wall just behind Juliette's shoulder.

"Liv... I can't even begin to express to you how sorry I am. There aren't enough words... what I did was despicable. I betrayed you. It was the worst thing I ever did in my life, and it makes me sick to remember how I treated you. I know I have no right to beg your forgiveness – and you have every right to tell me to go to hell – but I'm going to do it anyway. Please, Liv, will you forgive me?"

Something like hope flickered in Liv's eyes, and she finally looked at Juliette. "You're sorry?"

"Of course I am."

"Then come out to your mom."

"What?"

"You heard me. If you truly care about me, then you'll drop this charade – for both our sakes."

"Liv... I can't do that."

"Then, your apology means nothing."

"It does! Liv, I swear it does. I've never been sorrier for anything in my life –"

"Words! You give me sweet words, but your actions speak louder than your words – they scream, Juliette. They scream that you care more about keeping some dumb secret than you care more about me, about us."

"I love you," Juliette whispered. "Please, Liv, I love you."

"I don't believe you," Liv said flatly.

There was only one thing she could do to convince Liv, and that was the one thing Juliette couldn't do.

"Please, Liv, don't let it end like this," she begged. "I know you love me too."

Liv's expression took on a haunted look. "I did," she said softly. "At least, I loved who I thought you were. I was a fool. That woman doesn't exist."

Those words pierced Juliette's heart.

"Please, Juliette, just go. There is nothing more to say."

"I have to fight for us!"

"There's nothing left to fight for."

Juliette felt like she been punched in the stomach. Liv went to lie on her side in bed, facing away from Juliette. Juliette ached to comfort her, but Juliette was the last person Liv would want to accept comfort from right now.

She wandered through to her room in a daze.

It was over. It was really over.

How could she have fucked everything up so thoroughly?

There had to be a way to fix this.

There was, but it was one path Juliette couldn't take. She lay down on her side, imitating Liv's position, wrapping her arms around her knees.

Was it really so impossible? She can't be the first gay person in history faced with coming out to unsupportive parents. People all over the world did it every day, even knowing that they would be disowned and kicked out of the house, many in circumstances where their only recourse would be a homeless shelter or living on the streets.

That wasn't the case for Juliette. She had much better options. She wouldn't be left destitute – at least in terms of money.

But she would lose the only family she had. How could she do that? How could Liv ask that of her?

She could, because deep down, Juliette knew it was a fair request. Asking the woman she loved to live a lie wasn't reasonable. Asking someone to come out, even if they were consequences, was a reasonable requirement for dating them.

That knowledge didn't help her much, because Juliette still couldn't do it.

Juliette didn't know how she was going to get through one day without Liv, let alone the entire, desolate lifetime that was stretching out ahead of her.

She tried to focus on her work, but her work was crap right now. She'd had no trouble painting before she met Liv. Logically, she should still be able to find inspiration in her surroundings and her own thoughts.

It was like Liv had taken the life right out of her paintings, though. Juliette threw away canvas after canvas of utter crap. It was a nightmare. She had always loved her work, but now, even that had been taken from her.

Juliette tried to keep up the motions, all for the sake of her lie. She had sacrificed everything to keep this lie going. The last thing she was going to do was let her mom figure out what was going on, which meant hiding how thoroughly depressed she was.

Juliette got out of bed. She ate a balanced diet and got enough sleep. She tried her best to work on her paintings. From the outside, she was doing everything she needed to live a functioning life. She was coping.

Internally, Juliette was not coping. Her mind had become a relentless chasm of pain and loneliness. She wanted Liv so much her chest ached, but there was nothing she could do to assuage that pain.

It was made worse by the fact that they were still living together. That should have made it better – knowing that she still got to see Liv, but it actually just made Juliette sad every time she looked at her.

She missed their easy friendship. Liv hadn't just been Juliette's partner; she had been her best friend. In losing her, Juliette had not only lost a lover, but the best friend she'd ever had.

She's the love of my life.

Juliette felt her heart breaking.

It was going to come down to a choice between her Liv and her mother. It was an impossible choice to make. How did she even begin to weigh the pros and cons of such a decision. She loved Liv more than anything, more than life itself, but her mom was... well, her mom. Juliette couldn't imagine her life without her mom's love and support in it.

In desperation, she turned to the internet. It turned out that there were many support forums dealing with this exact issue.

Juliette read through posts and was not encouraged. Sure, there were a few stories about the parents miraculously accepting their gay children, but the vast majority of stories about people coming out to bigoted parents ended in disaster.

Years later, they were still estranged. How could she choose that for herself?

She found herself posting her story in a forum, a long paragraph explaining her dilemma. Juliette anxiously refreshed the screen, waiting for replies to come. When they did, they were a mixed bag.

Fuck your mom. If she doesn't accept you, she doesn't deserve you in her life.

If your gf is ready to break up with you for not coming out, she's not the one for you.

Find someone else who's willing to respect your secret.

Come out. It was worth it for me.

Coming out was the worst decision of my life. I've lost everything.

Juliette scrolled through the different comments, trying to determine which way the answer was leaning, but there were so many back and forth answers, she was no closer to making a decision than she had been when she posted here.

One comment in particular stuck with her.

In the end, you've got to decide what's more important to you – holding onto your future or holding onto your past. And only you and decide which is which. In the end, you'll have to do what your heart tells you.

That was the question, wasn't it? Was Liv her future, or her past? Was her mother's love her future, or her past? Juliette couldn't have both.

She wished with all her heart that she could, but it simply wasn't possible. She closed down the forum. She should have known better than to seek answers from the internet. What did some group of strangers know?

Juliette went back to her studio, determined to paint something halfway decent. She was rummaging around for a fresh canvas – she'd thrown away so many that she was running low – when she knocked an old painting over.

Juliette cringed as she saw what it was. The half-finished painting of Liv, naked on the couch.

Liv's eyes were as warm as her smile, and as beautiful.

Juliette clutched the painting to her chest and broke down in tears.

9

OLIVIA

It was like living in some weird alternate universe. On paper, everything was the same as before, when Juliette hadn't been a part of Liv's life.

She still spent most of her time working. She still had a close relationship with her dad. She was still friendly with the staff who worked for her. Her eating and sleeping habits remained much the same, and she was working hard to make sure she didn't fall apart in the self-care department. No one wanted to have to go into a meeting with a boss who hadn't been able to bring herself to shower that day.

On the outside, everything was the same.

However, in reality, nothing was the same.

Liv wasn't the same.

Loving Juliette had forever changed her, and Liv couldn't seem to bring back the pleasure and satisfaction she had felt in her life before she had known Juliette.

Even if she couldn't have her as a partner, Liv missed Juliette as a friend... but Juliette didn't truly care for her. If she did, she would put her money where her mouth was and come out. Liv wouldn't settle for a friend who she knew didn't care for her as much as Liv did. She was worth more than that.

Living with Juliette, though, was impossible. Seeing her every day, seeing what she wanted more than anything but couldn't have, was driving her crazy.

Liv remembered what she had told her father in the beginning. If things didn't work, she may have to move out.

Well, things certainly weren't working, and she didn't see how time was going to change anything. She needed a fresh start.

Liv considered finding another house or an apartment, somewhere close by, so that she could still get to work and see her father easily enough... but it wasn't enough.

Work wasn't the sanctuary it had once been. Memories of Juliette sitting in her office, handing her cheeseburgers, haunted her whenever she was there. She remembered kissing Juliette on the roof as they looked out over the city. Holding her hand when they walked through empty hallways and no one would see.

Liv needed more than a different house. She needed an entirely fresh start. Only that way could she pull her life back together.

"Dad, can we go out for supper tonight? Just the two of us?"

"Sure! That's a good idea. We haven't done that in a while."

"I'll see you after work, then."

"Liv, is everything ok?"

Liv bit her lip. She was so done with lying. "We'll talk tonight, ok?"

"Yeah, ok. Hang in there, honey."

She knew he knew, but they couldn't talk about it, not without triggering his obligation to tell Laura what he had been told. Baseless suspicions, he could keep to himself, but if it was confirmed... well, Liv didn't want to put him in that position.

Work, which had been dragging recently, suddenly flew by. Liv was nervous about the coming conversation, and of course, time did not cooperate in her wish to procrastinate. All too soon, she and her dad were sitting opposite each other in Joe's.

She was silent for so long that he felt the need to broach the subject. "So... are you going to tell me what's been eating at you the last couple of weeks?"

"It's complicated. I can't really get into it, but I do need to tell you something. I think I need a fresh start."

"Ok. What does a fresh start look like to you?"

Liv braced herself. "I want to move to Europe and start a branch of Aimee Enterprises over there."

Her father recoiled as though she had struck him. "Liv, honey, surely there has to be another way. You and Juliette must be able to work this out somehow."

Liv considered denying that Juliette was the reason for her sudden desire to change continents, but what would be the point? Kane knew, that much was obvious.

"There really isn't. Trust me, if there was any hope whatsoever, I would be staying. I need to go, Dad."

Kane sighed. "I understand, Liv. I wish you would stay, but of course, you need to do what works best for you. You've done amazingly as CEO here. I'm sure you'll be equally successful in your new venture. I will of course give you any support you require to make it work."

Liv felt her eyes brimming with tears. She'd gone into this meeting not knowing what to expect. She should have known better. Of course, her dad would support her. When had he ever been anything but understanding and supportive?

"Thank you, dad," she said thickly. "You'll come visit me, right?"

"Of course. We'll make plans to see each other as often as we can, and for the in between times – well, that's what Zoom is for, isn't it?"

Liv nodded, still fighting back tears. They would work something out, but it wouldn't be the same. It would never be the same again. She'd been so focused on escaping her pain, the pain that flared every time she saw Juliette, that she hadn't really taken time to consider just how much she'd be losing by going.

She still had to go; there was no question about that. Living like this was untenable. However, she knew that starting anew in a different country would be far from easy. This was a hard road she had chosen, and the fact that she didn't have any other real options wouldn't make it any easier.

"I'll miss you."

Her dad moved around the table so that he could put an arm around her. "I'll miss you too, Liv. Try not to fret. We've been through worse than this together before. We can get through this, too. I… is there any way I could convince you to stay? If Juliette moved out…"

"No," Liv said sharply. "I'm not chasing Juliette out of her home."

No matter what had happened between them, Liv still loved Juliette. That wasn't the kind of thing you could turn off. She didn't want her departure to hurt the woman she loved. Besides, if her dad asked Juliette to move out, that would surely lead to questions, and Liv didn't want that.

Juliette had made it clear that protecting her sexuality from her mother was more important than anything. Liv wasn't going to participate in outing her, even in the most indirect way.

"Alright. I don't want to cause trouble for either of you. I just wish there was something I could do to help."

"You're already doing it. Your support means the world to me, Dad."

"You have that, Liv. Always."

Liv had been braced for anything – anger, disappointment, even refusal to allow her to use the company name in her new venture. If anything, her father's support only made her feel guiltier about the coming move.

Ever since her mom died, they had only had each other. Now, she was leaving him. The thought left a bitter taste in her mouth, but what else could she do? Keep living like this? Impossible. If she ever wanted to find happiness, she had to go.

Liv didn't delude herself. There would be no finding love again. Juliette had been it for her. She wasn't ever going to move on, wasn't ever going to recover from the wound Juliette had left on her heart.

However, she could learn to live with it. Liv hoped that she could find solace in her work and learn to be happy alone again. She would make new friends, and find her new work family. The thought seemed hollow comfort now, but surely, with time, it would get easier.

"Please don't tell Juliette and Laura – at least not yet. wait until I'm gone. I don't want goodbyes."

"Goodbyes might be good for you. They would give you some closure.

"I don't think so. It'll only make everything worse."

"As you wish. I'm telling them once you're gone, though. I won't keep this from Laura forever – not like I could even keep it from her in the first place, once you've left."

"I know. Tell her that I needed a fresh start."

That much was true. There was no reason to give out the reason for this sudden desire for a new beginning.

"I'll tell her... tell them both. When do you plan on leaving?"

"As soon as I can get my things together. There will be a lot of admin to do, but I can do that from the other side. I'll stay in a hotel until I can find a place to live. I don't know how long it'll take to get a license to start a business there, but I'll figure it out."

"It may be easier to sort things out from this end, rather than throw yourself into the deep end, getting to a foreign country and then having to start with an admin nightmare."

"I know. It would be easier, but I can't... I just want to go as soon as possible."

Her father's eyes were full of concern as he looked at her. Liv feared he would question her further, but to her relief, he didn't.

"You should take Meg with you. It'll be good to have a familiar face with you, and she'll be brilliant with helping you sort out the details."

"What makes you think Meg wants to move to Europe?"

"If you go to Belgium, she will."

Oh yes. Liv had forgotten about that. Meg had a long distance boyfriend in Belgium who she had been with for three years. They visited when they could, but flights from Europe to the US were expensive.

Liv knew that Meg had talked about moving to Belgium, but finding a job there was difficult. If Meg agreed, it should actually work out perfectly.

"That's a great idea. Belgium it is. I'll talk to Meg in the morning. She's going to be thrilled."

'Thrilled' didn't' even begin to cover it. Meg was ecstatic. Liv gave her the morning off, supposedly to call Alex, but really, it was to give Meg some time to calm down. She was too full of excited energy to settle to anything, let alone work.

This had been a great idea. It was impossible not to pick up some of Meg's enthusiasm. Liv had always liked a challenge, and this would be one of the biggest challenges in her career. She was sure she could make it work, and couldn't stop thinking about how satisfying it would be to create something entirely her own, something she had achieved without her father by her side.

Liv loved working with her father, and she didn't resent the fact that almost everything they had accomplished had been a team effort. However, she found the idea of succeeding with nothing but her own talents to back her up enticing.

Of course, it wouldn't be a completely solo venture. She would have company funds to help her get started, and she would of course rely on her dad's experience and advice. However, she would be on her own in more ways than she ever had been before.

"When do we leave?"

Meg's voice broke Liv out of her thoughts. "Oh. Well, how soon can you be ready to leave?"

"I can get my stuff packed by tonight."

Liv chuckled. "Hold your horses. It's going to take me at least a few days to get everything ready."

She would probably be able to get her stuff

packed sooner, except she wanted to do it sneakily. She didn't want Juliette to know until she was already gone. Perhaps it was cowardly, but Liv didn't want to face final goodbyes.

Once she was gone, who knew if she would ever see Juliette again? Sure, she'd visit home, but that didn't mean she and Juliette would necessarily run into each other.

The thought of never seeing Juliette again was like a punch to the gut, but Liv reminded herself that this was what she wanted. A fresh start, away from heartache and loneliness. She was sure that those emotions would follow her to some extent, but she'd have Meg with her and the challenge of starting a new business to keep her busy.

"Liv? Are you alright?"

"What? Oh yes, I'm fine. Just thinking."

"This is definitely happening, right? You're not going to change your mind?"

"I would never do that to you, Meg. I wouldn't have offered you this opportunity if I wasn't sure. We're going to live in Belgium."

Meg squealed in excitement – for about the fourth time today – and ran to hug Liv. "I can't believe it! What made you decide on Belgium?"

"Honestly? I wanted you to come with me to

Europe, and I figured that if I picked Belgium, it would be an offer you couldn't refuse."

"You're right about that. You just wait, Liv – this is going to be epic. I'll handle everything. You'll barely have any work to do."

Liv didn't doubt that Meg could kick that admin in the ass, but she did need to keep busy. She was sure that while Meg could do it alone, she would also be grateful for the help.

"Alex says you're welcome to stay with us until you find your own place."

Oh. Liv hadn't expected that. "I'd really appreciate that. I think it'll be a lot easier if I start off living with people I know."

Liv could easily afford to get a solo place, but she was toying with the idea of finding a room-mate. She had never lived alone and she wasn't sure if she wanted to. She was going to be lonely enough; no need to add to that.

"You can stay as long as you need. I'm sure we'll all get along just fine. Alex is great, you'll see."

"I'm sure he is." Excitement was curling in Liv's belly. "This is going to be great."

"I hope you like cats."

Liv sighed. "How many does he have now?"

"He just adopted his seventh."

She had to laugh. "Are you sure there will be space for both of us along with all the cats?"

"Don't worry about it – he still lives in his family home, even though his sisters moved out a couple of years ago. He has plenty of space."

"Well, I do like cats. I'm sure I'll be fine there."

Liv had always wanted a cat, but her dad was allergic. Thankfully, she hadn't inherited that trait. Maybe when she was living alone, she could adopt a cat herself if the roommate thing didn't work out.

"Do you have any idea what the process is in terms of starting a business in Belgium?"

"Not yet, but I'll find out. Alex will know all the ins and outs. He'll be able to help us get started."

Liv knew that Alex had started several successful businesses of his own in Belgium.

"I hope he's not going to poach you from me."

Meg laughed. "You don't need to worry about that. I have no desire to work for him. That would just make things way too complicated. It's better to keep work and personal lives separate."

"You'll have to stop working such long hours, if you want to spend any time with him."

"Bah, he works even longer hours than I do. We'll be fine, Liv."

Meg didn't ask her about her sudden desire to move to Europe, and Liv was grateful, but a little exasperated. Honestly, did *everyone* know about her and Juliette? She had thought they were being subtle, but apparently, their subtlety was wasted on everyone except Laura.

Liv supposed that Laura's ignorance was what mattered. It wasn't like anyone else in her life would judge them. Laura might have figured it out too if it wasn't something she really didn't want to see.

"I suppose I'd better let you go – I'm sure you want to start packing."

"If it's going to be a few days anyway, then I should work for now. I'll pack after work. There's so much to do – closing things up here, finding a new CEO, getting flights arranged…"

Yeah, bringing Meg was definitely the right decision. Liv would have been completely over-whelmed without her. She could have handled it alone if necessary, but she was glad she didn't have to.

"Which language do you want to learn?"

"What?"

"Well, the official languages are Dutch, French

and German. Alex is bilingual in English and French, so I'll be learning French."

"I hadn't thought of that."

"I mean, it's not essential. Most everyone will speak English, at least in the big cities like where we'll be moving. But we'll have a better chance of getting citizenship in a few years if we're fluent in one of their languages."

"That's a good point. I hadn't thought that far ahead, but you're right. It'll make our lives a lot easier to know at least one of the languages. I'm not sure I want to give up my US citizenship, though."

"Me neither – I'm going to look into dual citizenship. I can do the same for you. Should I start arranging lessons for us? Alex can help by speaking French to us at home, but we should go for formal lessons, too, and he won't have much free time to teach us."

"That would be perfect. I'll download some apps in the meantime so that I can get started. I suppose we should start testing each other on vocabulary."

"Damn right. We're going to kick this thing in the butt."

Liv spent the rest of the day making arrangements. She was dreading telling the rest of the staff, who were unlikely to be nearly as enthusiastic as Meg was, but it was better to do it now before they found out by themselves.

So, Liv called an informal meeting at the end of the day, gathering everyone in the main work area.

"Hi, everyone. I have news, but before I give it, let me just assure you that your jobs are safe. Nothing much is going to change for all of you... but I'm leaving."

Dismayed murmurs filled the room, but Liv soldiered on. "I'm going to Belgium to start a new branch of Aimee Enterprises. My dad will fill in as CEO until we can find a permanent replacement. Meg is coming with me, and if any of you would like to find a fresh start in Europe, I'll gladly help with your moving expenses. However, I don't expect any of you to move continents with me, so please don't feel like you need to in order to keep your jobs. I'll struggle to replace such an excellent group of people, and your new CEO will be lucky to have you."

"Why, Liv?" Harriet, their accounts lady, looked distraught. "I thought you were happy here?"

"I am. This place has been like a second home

to me… but there are other factors involved. It's not anything to do with work, I promise."

A couple of people exchanged knowing looks. For fuck's sake, was she that bad at keeping a secret? Liv gritted her teeth and pretended not to notice the looks. "Meg and I will probably leave toward the end of the week. I'll throw us all a farewell party before we go."

She'd also make sure to give everyone substantial bonuses for all their good work, but Liv would save that to be a surprise.

She spent a little more time in the office, answering questions and reassuring anyone who was anxious about the coming change.

Liv finally returned home, wishing she could stay at work longer, just to avoid the wrench of pain seeing Juliette brought every time Liv laid eyes on her. However, she had stuff to do. She had already rented a storage unit to start sneakily moving her stuff to. Once she had everything assembled – taking it out in dribs and drabs – she would pack it all into a couple of suitcases and head off to the airport with Meg.

Despite her heartache, Liv was filled with excitement at the thought of this new chapter in her life. She may never truly recover from Juliette, but that didn't mean she wouldn't take whatever happiness she was still capable of having.

This was going to be a new start for her, and she couldn't wait.

The days were much the same. Wake up. Force herself to shower and eat. Try and fail to paint. Lunch. Try to paint again. Mope. Do her best not to cry. Splash some paint onto canvas and throw the canvas away in a fit of frustration. Dinner. Sleep, dreaming of Liv.

Juliette was sick of the dull, dreary thing her life had become, but she didn't know any way out of this miserable existence.

She was trying, she really was. Juliette had been happy before Liv came into her life. Logically, she should be able to be happy again. After all, her life didn't look any different to before Liv had entered it.

Juliette was different, though. Liv had changed her, and she wasn't sure if she could ever go back. She tried to take comfort in the fact that she still had her mother's love. Ever since she was young, she and Laura had been all the other had.

Now Laura had Kane, but she and Juliette were still close.

Juliette wished she could confide in her mom, but that simply wasn't possible.

It was late when she got home from the grocery store. She had been procrastinating leaving, wanting to wait for Liv to be home before she got back.

Liv had been working later and later recently, but it was already dark. She should be home soon. As much as seeing Liv hurt, it was better to hurt than not see her at all. The memories were bitter-sweet, but being without Liv was just bitter.

When Juliette arrived home, she was pleased to see Liv's car in the driveway. She walked inside, going to the kitchen to pack the groceries away.

Liv wasn't there, but Laura was, working over the stove. The enticing aroma of stir fry filled the room.

"Hey, Juliette. Thanks for the groceries. Why

don't you set the table? Kane said he'll be working late, so it's just the two of us tonight."

Juliette frowned. "Where's Liv? Was she going out for dinner?" Why, then, was her car in the driveway?

Laura sighed. "Let's go to the lounge." She turned the stove off. "We need to talk."

Juliette's breath caught in her throat. Those words were never followed by anything good. There was only one thing she could think of that could bring such a serious expression to her mom's face.

She knew. Fuck, she was about to kick Juliette out of the house, wasn't she? Juliette did her best not to hyperventilate as different options spun through her head. She could try to deny it, but she had no idea what kind of evidence Laura had against her. She could promise to change, but Juliette knew that would be a lie.

Like it or not, she was thoroughly gay, and her sexuality wasn't going anywhere.

She sat down on the sofa, clasping her hands to hide how hard they were trembling.

"Liv is gone."

Oh shit. Laura wasn't kicking Juliette out of the house – she was kicking *Liv* out of the house. Of course, Laura would blame Liv for 'corrupting'

Juliette. It would be easier than blaming Juliette. But how could Kane allow her to chase his own daughter from her home?

"You can't – this is Liv's home. It's my fault. I'll go. Leave Liv be."

Laura frowned. "What are you talking about?"

Juliette's certainty ebbed. "What are *you* talking about?"

"Juliette, Liv has decided to move to Europe. She's starting a new branch of Aimee Enterprises there."

A whole new kind of panic filled Juliette, so intense that she could barely breathe. "What?" she whispered. "Liv... Liv's gone?"

"She just left a few hours ago."

"No – no, she can't." Juliette felt tears spring to her eyes as she clutched at the arms of the sofa, trying to hold onto something steady as her world spun on its axis. Would she ever see Liv again? Juliette couldn't stand the thought of living without Liv beside her.

"I'm sorry, sweetie. I know how close the two of you were." Laura came to put an arm around Juliette's shoulders.

Juliette blinked dumbly at her mother. "You don't understand."

"I know it's hard – losing a friend always is – but you two can still keep in touch. And I'm sure Liv will be back to visit –"

"No, you don't understand!" Juliette realized she was on her feet. She shouldn't shout, but she controlling her voice was the last thing on her mind right now.

"Juliette, don't distress yourself. You have other friends. You can –"

"Liv isn't just a friend! I love her, mom!"

"Of course you do. I love her too. I'm sure she'll always be like a sister to you, but sometimes, family moves away and –"

"No, you don't get it! I don't just love her. I'm *in love* with her!"

Laura's eyes narrowed dangerously. "I'm afraid I don't follow."

Juliette hesitated. She could backtrack. She could claim she had misspoken, and Laura would believe her, because that's what she wanted to believe.

But Juliette couldn't do this, not anymore. She couldn't bear to lose Liv. Not like this. Not when there was anything she could do about it. Maybe it was far too late, but she had to try. She had to fight for the woman she loved.

That meant doing the thing that terrified her most... but Juliette realized that now that it had come down to a choice, she chose Liv. She may lose her mother forever, but she needed Liv more than she needed anyone or anything else.

"I'm gay, mom. Liv and I are together. I'm in love with her. I want to marry her. I want to have children with her. She's the love of my life."

Laura's expression was thunderous. "Think about what you're saying, Juliette. I know you're upset, but that's no reason to overreact. I know you love Liv, but I think you're confusing familial love with something... else."

"No, I'm not. I know what I feel. Making love to Liv feels right, which is more than I can say about any man I've been with. This is who I am, mom."

"No, it's not," Laura hissed from behind clenched teeth. "No daughter of mine will be gay! I intend to see you in heaven, Juliette. Don't you dare make it otherwise."

Juliette felt like her mom had slapped her. It would have been better if she had. The tears spilled over. "I'm not going to hell," she whispered.

"Damn right you're not, because we're going to get you some proper help. There are some excellent facilities..."

A conversion camp. Her mom wanted to send her to a conversion camp.

Of course, Laura never would have accepted her. Juliette had known that, but that didn't make it hurt any less. She hadn't thought her heart could become any more broken and mangled than it already was, but she had been wrong.

"Juliette? What's going – oh. Laura told you."

Juliette looked up at Kane with pleading eyes. Surely, he would stand up for her. Juliette had stood up for gay rights to her mother multiple times, but now, she couldn't even bring herself to look Laura in the eye.

"Oh." His face softened in sympathy. "Laura told you about Liv."

"Liv? Do you have any idea what your daughter has done, Kane? Juliette's eternal soul is in danger because of Olivia's actions!"

Kane folded his arms. "What are you talking about?"

Juliette suspected he knew exactly what she was talking about, but he clearly wanted her to spell it out.

"Olivia has got Juliette thinking she's gay."

"I *am* gay, mom! And that's not Liv's fault. I

would have figured it out sooner or later, Liv or no Liv."

"You're not really gay, Juliette. You're just confused."

"Laura, be reasonable. Juliette knows her own mind and body."

"But she can't be – I won't lose my daughter!"

"She's right there!" Kane gestured angrily to Juliette. "You're not losing her!"

"But her soul –"

"Oh, you can fuck right off with that Leviticus crap, Laura! It's a bunch of bullshit and you know it!"

Laura gaped at him like a goldfish. Kane had never spoken so harshly to her in their entire relationship. "But... but..."

"But nothing. You call yourself a Christian? Then be like fucking Christ, Laura! Anything else and you're not a Christian, you're just a hypocrite. Tell me truthfully, what would Jesus say?"

"He'd tell her to repent –"

"No, he wouldn't! Have you even read the Bible, Mom? He'd tell me that my father in Heaven loves me unconditionally."

"Yes, but –"

"There are no buts. Either you accept me or

you don't, but don't you dare pretend you're forsaking me because that's what Jesus wants you to do. Juliette stormed over the book shelf and withdrew a copy of the Bible. She hurled it at Laura, who had to duck to avoid it.

"Go re-read the fucking gospel!" Juliette snapped. Then she stalked out of the room, half-blinded by tears. She made it to her room and fell into bed, pressing her face into the pillow to muffle her sobs.

She could hear Kane and Laura screaming at each other in the lounge. Juliette was distantly gratified that Kane had stood up for her when she hadn't been able to stand up for herself, but that did little to outweigh the anguish she felt at her mother's rejection.

Juliette had known it was coming, of course, and she had thought she'd be prepared for how much it would hurt.

She was wrong. She hadn't been prepared for this at all.

She didn't know how much time had passed – two tissue boxes worth – before there was a knock on the door.

Juliette resisted the urge to scream at Kane to go away. He was worried and checking in on her.

She didn't want company right now, but the least she could do was tell that to him to his face.

"Yes?"

The door opened. "Juliette."

Juliette was shocked to hear her mom's voice.

"Go away," Juliette snapped. "You can take your intolerance and your conversion camps and you can go straight to hell."

"That's not what I'm here for. I want... I want to apologize."

Juliette didn't dare hope. "Let me guess. Kane told you that you had to treat me right or he'd leave you."

Laura glared at her. "Kane loves me. He would never give me an ultimatum like that. However, he did help me... see certain things better."

"Oh yeah?" Juliette couldn't imagine that Kane had said anything different to what she'd been telling her mom her whole life. But maybe it would be different coming from her fiancé. Juliette knew that Liv probably had a better chance of convincing her to do something she didn't want to do than anyone else. Perhaps it was the same for their parents?

"Juliette... I won't pretend to be happy about this, but you're right. Rejecting you is not what

Jesus would do. I'm... I'm going to try to be better. You're gay, and I love you. I'll get used to the idea. I just need a bit of time. Can you grant me that?"

Juliette eyed her suspiciously, wondering if this was some kind of long con to get her into a conversion camp. "How do I know you really mean that?"

"I know I need to prove myself to you. I failed spectacularly as a mother at your coming out, but I can be better. Perhaps this will start to prove to you that I really do intend to try."

Laura took out a folded piece of paper and handed it to Juliette. Juliette scanned it, her eyes widening as she read.

"A plane ticket to Belgium?"

"You go get your girl."

She stared at Laura for several seconds, hardly able to believe it. "You... you want me and Liv to be together?"

"I want you to be happy. If that's with Liv..." Laura took a deep breath. "... then that's what I want for you. The idea is going to take some getting used to, but that's my problem, not yours. I promise, you won't be exposed to any more bigotry from me. Kane has already found me a support group for family members of queer people who are struggling with their situations. I think – no, I know – that I can get this right."

The paper fluttered to the floor as Juliette flung her arms around her mother. "I love you, mom," she sobbed.

Laura hugged her tightly back. "I love you too, Juliette. But there's time for that later. Your and Liv's flight leaves in less than an hour. I suggest that you hurry."

With no time to pack anything, Juliette grabbed her ticket and flew from the room.

"Alex already has a room prepared for you. He's so excited to meet you."

"That sounds great, Meg." Liv tried to match Meg's enthusiasm, but she didn't quite manage it. Meg babbled on excitedly, and Liv did her best to pay attention to it, but her heavy heart cast a pall over everything. It was like hearing and seeing through a layer of thick fog.

The fog of despair surrounded Liv, leaving her feeling isolated, even though the room was full of people.

As much as she was looking forward to the new life she would be starting, right now, she too busy grieving the life she'd be leaving behind to feel much anticipation.

She would miss her father, friends and colleagues, to be sure, but most of all, she would miss Juliette.

The others, she could keep in contact with. She and Juliette weren't even speaking. Once Liv left, this was it. In all likelihood she wouldn't ever see Juliette again. Never hear her voice or touch her lips...

"Liv? Liv, are you there?"

"I'm here," Liv mumbled, forcing herself to look at Meg.

"Are you sure this is the right decision? You look like you're about to collapse. I'm sure if you just talked to Juliette –"

"We've said everything there is to say. This is the only way. Besides, don't you want to go?"

"More than anything. But I also don't want you to be unhappy. Do you really think you'll find what you're looking for in Belgium?"

What she was looking for was a way to escape the memories of her too-brief time with Juliette. Would Belgium offer that?

"I don't know. I have to try something, though. I can't keep living like this. It's not a life, Meg."

Meg sighed. "I understand. I'm sorry things can't be different."

Liv blinked back tears. "Me too, Meg. Me too."

"We're boarding. Come on. You can do this."

They got into the line for boarding.

"Liv! Liv, wait!"

For a moment, Liv thought she was going mad, imagining Juliette's voice, calling her back. But then Meg turned around, and Liv followed her gaze.

There was Juliette, her face red and blotchy, but her blue eyes blazing with passion as she pushed her way through the crowd, waving frantically at Liv.

What was she doing here? She was just going to make this harder on both of them; did she not know that? Perhaps Juliette thought that a goodbye would give her closure, but for Liv, it would just add more pain.

It was too late to prevent that now, though. She stepped out of the line, resigned to having this one last conversation with Juliette.

"Liv!"

Juliette skidded to a stop in front of her.

"Yes, Juliette?"

"I love you."

Liv grimaced. "I love you too, Juliette. Not that it changes anything."

"Yes, it does! It changes everything. Liv, I was so stupid before. Letting you go was the dumbest thing I've ever done in my life. I can't take it back, but I can do my best to correct it."

"Juliette, there's nothing to correct. We can't go back. I've already told you, I won't live a lie. You –"

"I came out to my mom."

Liv dropped her suitcase painfully on her foot. Meg snatched it up, leaving Liv's toe throbbing, but she barely noticed it. "You... came out to your mom?"

"Yeah, I did. She wasn't happy at first, but she promises that she's going to work harder on acceptance. I think she'll get there eventually, but even if she doesn't... well, I choose you, Liv. I'd rather have you than her. You're all I need, all I want. Please, Liv, will you take me back?"

Liv was still reeling from that little sentence, so small and yet so meaningful. *I came out to my mom.*

She wanted more than anything to take Juliette into her arms and kiss her, but that would only make it harder on both of them when they had to part. "Juliette... I'm moving to Europe. I'm sorry, but I don't have it in me to do the long distance thing. We couldn't –"

"No, you don't understand. I know you're moving to Europe... and I'm coming with you."

It was a good thing Meg already had Liv's suitcase, because she was sure she would have dropped it again. "You... what?"

"I'm coming with you to Europe. I understand if you can't forgive me yet. I can wait. I'll rent my own place, and I'll earn your trust, bit by bit. I'll do whatever it takes. The only thing I won't do is give up on you – on us. We have something precious, Liv – too precious to lose. I'm sorry it took me so long to see that."

Liv stared at Juliette, the most beautiful woman she had ever met. Was this divine creature truly offering her everything she had ever wanted, or was this some cruel dream, taunting her while hard reality got ready to thrash her when she woke up?

"Liv? Please, say something."

If this was a dream, Liv would take it.

She was lost for words. Instead of trying to find the right ones, she stepped forward and pulled Juliette into her arms. Their lips met in a kiss that was both tentative and sweet. Liv could feel the joy and triumph radiating from Juliette as they kissed.

The need to be sure had Liv pulling back. "Are you certain about this, Juliette? Moving to Europe is a big deal. Is this truly what you want?"

"I want to be with you. I don't care what part of the world that's in. Besides, I hear Belgium has great chocolate. How bad can it really be if we have world-class chocolate to come home to at the end of the day?"

Liv couldn't help it. She laughed. "Yeah, there is that."

"So you'll take me?"

"Oh, Juliette, of course I will. You're all I want as well."

"If you two are done, we'd best get boarding, or we're going to miss our flight," Meg pointed out.

"Right!" Liv saw that the flight attendants were eyeing them impatiently. There was no more line; everyone else had boarded.

Liv took Juliette's hand. "Do you not have any hand luggage?"

"No luggage at all. I didn't have time to pack."

"So you're going to a foreign country with nothing more than your purse and the clothes you're wearing?"

Juliette shrugged. "I can buy new clothes there." She took Liv's hand and squeezed it. "Everything I need is right here."

"Yeah, yeah, come on, you two saps. If we miss this flight, there isn't another one for six hours."

Liv couldn't resist kissing Juliette once more before turning to follow a very smug-looking Meg onto the plane.

She and Juliette stepped into the aisle holding hands.

Liv still couldn't believe it. The fog of despair was gone, banished so thoroughly that she had trouble even remembering what it had felt like. Her heart was lighter than air as she and Juliette took their seats. Juliette swapped with someone so that they could sit together. Meg was grinning almost as widely as Juliette and Liv. Liv knew that Meg was relieved everything had worked out so wonderfully – though not as relieved as she was.

All the excitement Liv had felt at the thought of branching out her business resurfaced, somehow multiplied tenfold now that she knew Juliette would be there with her through it all.

"I can't believe you came out to her for me."

"I'd do anything for you, Liv. It just took me a while to realize that."

"You really think she'll accept you? Accept us?"

"She wouldn't have bought me this plane ticket if she wasn't serious about trying."

"She bought the plane ticket?"

"Yeah. I mean, I was planning on coming after you anyway, but I was so upset that I probably would have taken a few days to calm down and followed you when I was more stable. But she gave me the ticket, and I knew it would be better to catch you now, before you left."

"I'm glad you did. I don't know how I would have survived, knowing that I was leaving you for good."

"Well, now you'll never need to find out."

"Yeah," Liv sighed happily, putting an arm around Juliette's shoulders. "I don't want to live without you again."

"You won't have to. I'm not going to live like I was – living in fear that my mom might find out who I truly am. From now on, I'm going to live my life in love, not in fear."

"Not in fear," Liv agreed.

If this was a dream, Liv prayed that she never woke up.

EPILOGUE
JULIETTE- 2 YEARS LATER

"Juliette. Breathe. Liv is waiting for you. You're going to be fine."

"Liv." Juliette forced herself to think of her fiancé – her wife, in less than half an hour.

"That's right, Liv. Now come on. The music is starting. I'll have none of this fashionably late business from my own daughter."

Juliette nodded, clutching her mom's arm. Laura walked her steadily down the aisle, setting a slow pace that Juliette never would have managed on her own. As she rounded the corner, she saw Kane just finishing his own walk with Liv, kissing her on the cheek before going taking his place in the front row.

Juliette's eyes were on Liv from the moment she turned to face her. They had agreed not to look at each other's outfits until the wedding, but as she missed a step at the sight of Liv, Juliette suddenly wondered if that had been a good idea.

Thankfully, Laura's arm was there, helping her to balance. She righted herself, letting her eyes feast on Liv. Her Liv. Beautiful, amazing Olivia Jones- soon to be her wife.

Liv wore fitted pants in charcoal grey and a soft pink blouse. She looked incredible.

Juliette wore a soft pink dress. The clouds of chiffon and lace billowed around her, making her feel ethereal in the evening light. The dress was fitted from her bust down to her hips before flaring out into a wide skirt.

She felt like a princess.

The look in Liv's eyes made her feel like the most beautiful woman in the world. Liv looked at Juliette like she wanted to devour her where she stood. Juliette felt herself blushing as she imagined Liv taking this dress off her... but that wasn't a thought she should be having now, not if she wanted to focus on the ceremony.

Laura placed her hand in Liv's, beaming at both of them. Liv winked at Juliette before turning with her to face the pastor.

Juliette tried, she really did, but she kept losing track of the ceremony. The pastor spoke of love and devotion, of steadfastness and loyalty. All of them were things that Juliette associated with the wonderful woman next to her.

She was drifting in bliss when the pastor's words broke her out of her happy daze. "And now, the couple will make their vows to each other."

Juliette had a moment of panic as her vows fled her mind – but then she looked at Liv, and of course, she could remember her vows. Making promises of eternal love and devotion was as easy as breathing when Liv was the one she was promising herself to.

They faced each other and joined hands.

"Liv. When you came into my life, you showed me not only who I truly am, but what I was missing in my life. You're everything I've ever wanted, and I'm so lucky that you feel the same way about me.

"I promise that as your wife, I will support you in all your endeavors. I will stand by you through thick and through thin. Whatever struggles we face, we will do so together. I will always listen to you and believe in you. And most importantly, I promise to love you, until my dying breath."

Liv's eyes were sparkling as she squeezed Juliette's hands.

"Juliette. When I met you, I was struck by your beauty. It didn't take much time in getting to know you before I was also struck by your beautiful mind and heart. You are the love of my life, and every inch of ground we've had to fight for in order to be together is worth it. I promise to remind you to laugh at the little things when you're feeling down. I promise to accept you as you are, always. I'll always encourage you in your goals and dreams. And I swear that you will forever be my heart."

Juliette blinked back tears as Meg handed them the rings. She was hit by a sudden, irrational fear that the rings wouldn't fit, but of course, she and Liv had tried them on just a couple of days ago. Juliette's ring slid easily onto her finger, firm but not too tight. She put Liv's ring on, staring down at their joined hands for a few moments before looking up into Liv's eyes. Juliette felt like she could get lost forever in those eyes, and it was only the pastor's voice breaking through into the cloud of happiness surrounding her that got to look away.

"Then in the eyes of God and these witnesses, I pronounce you married! You may kiss."

Juliette melted into the kiss. She'd had many amazing kisses with Liv, from sweet to hot, gentle to rough, and everything in between.

It was like she was kissing her for the first time. The feeling of Liv's lips on hers sent a thrill of pleasure through Juliette's body. Liv's arms wrapping around her waist made her feel safe and so content that she never wanted to move.

When they finally broke apart, their guests were cheering for them. "I love you," Juliette whispered.

"I love you, Juliette."

Liv took her hand and together, they walked down the aisle.

There was food and dancing, and no small number of stolen kisses. The photographer followed them around like a faithful labrador, documenting every moment. Juliette knew that she would appreciate this later, but right now, all she wanted was to be alone with Liv.

Fortunately, the flight from Belgium to Italy

was only about two hours. They would be in their hotel room before midnight.

They were getting changed into their traveling clothes when there was a knock on the door. Juliette's mom stepped in, holding a wrapped parcel.

"I thought I'd give you your wedding gift before you left. I know you're only planning to open most of them when you get back, but I just didn't want to wait."

"Thanks, Mom." Juliette carefully unwrapped the package, to find a beautifully made, leather-bound photo album. Her breath caught as she flicked through the pages.

Pages and pages of pictures of her and Liv. Juliette hadn't even realized that her mom had been photographing half of these moments. Now that she thought about it, Laura did always seem to have her phone in her hand when Liv was around. She'd been taking pictures of them this whole time.

"Mom, this is..."

"Perfect," Liv finished. "It's utterly perfect. Thank you, Laura."

"I'm so proud of both of you, my daughters. I know I didn't exactly make it easy for you in the beginning, but you were patient with me and helped me grow, and I've become a better person for it."

"We're proud of you too, Mom. You worked so hard to become the person you are, and Liv and I both appreciate it."

"Yeah, we do. I'm so glad to have you in my life, Laura."

The three of them hugged tightly before breaking apart. "We should go." Juliette glanced at the clock. "We don't want to miss our flight."

The flight was as short as promised, but it felt like forever to Juliette. She had waited all day. She wanted to get her hands on her sexy wife, and she wanted it now.

"Almost there," Liv murmured, grinning as Juliette twitched in her seat.

She was far too composed for Juliette's liking.

Juliette leaned in close, placing her mouth over Liv's ear so that none of the other passengers could hear them.

"When we get to that hotel, I'm going to fuck you so good, Liv. You'll be in the middle of coming when hotel security bursts into the room because they think I'm murdering you, you'll scream so loud for me."

"What are you doing?" Liv hissed. "Do you

want me to embarrass myself? My panties are only so thick, you know."

"Get those panties soaked for me, Liv. Think of me fingering you, rubbing on your G-spot. I want to see a wet spot on your pants from you fantasizing about me fingering you over and over again until you squirt for me."

Liv moaned, her eyes slipping shut. "You're mean."

"Do you want me to stop?"

"Fuck no. Keep going."

Their sex life had gone from strength to strength. Juliette had found a raw sexuality within herself, she had had no idea had existed before Liv. But Liv drove her crazy with lust.

By the time the plane landed, Liv and Juliette were both near frenzied with need. Juliette reflected that it was a double-edged sword she was wielding, because while her words were certainly affecting Liv, they were affecting her just as much.

By the time they were in the uber on the way to the hotel, their restraint was cracking.

Juliette wasn't sure who initiated the kiss. She was sure that she was the one to climb into Liv's lap and start rutting against her thigh.

"Ladies! Can you save that for the hotel, please?"

"We're newlyweds," Juliette grumbled, but got off Liv anyway.

It didn't help matters much. Liv glanced at the uber driver before sneaking a hand over to Juliette's lap, slipping her fingers past Juliette's waistband and into her panties.

Juliette bit her lip to prevent herself from crying out as Liv's fingers brushed over her swollen clit. Liv started rubbing, so slowly that it was delicious torture to her already-inflamed body.

Juliette had to put all her concentration into keeping quiet, sure that they would be kicked out onto the street if their driver saw what they were doing. Liv carefully removed her hand as they arrived at the hotel, paying the driver and grabbing Juliette by the hand.

They eagerly handed their suitcases over to hotel staff and practically sprinted for their room. They could sort out the suitcases later. For now, the honeymoon suite was waiting for them.

They started stripping each other's clothes off in the elevator. Thankfully, it was late enough that they didn't bump into anyone.

Liv had the presence of mind to scoop their

clothes up and carry them into the suite. The huge bed looked very comfortable, but Juliette didn't think she was going to make it that far. She was all for making love right here on this thick carpet, but it seemed that Liv had other ideas.

She dropped the clothes and scooped Juliette up into her arms, carrying her to the bed and laying her down atop the puffy blankets.

"Liv, I need –"

Liv silenced her with a kiss. "I know. Let me take care of you, my love."

She didn't say anything else, because her tongue was suddenly very busy. Liv laved her tongue over Juliette's clit, just the way she knew Juliette liked it. She should probably last longer, but Liv had already gotten her so worked up in the uber that Juliette was about to explode.

Less than a minute later, she stiffened, grabbing Liv's head and pushing it down, moving it to get her clit at just the perfect angle.

"Oh yes, Liv, yes!"

Juliette's world narrowed down to a single point of blinding pleasure as she came on her wife's tongue.

Liv pulled away as Juliette came down, licking her lips. "You taste delicious, as always."

Juliette grinned. "Lie back."

She was still out of breath, but she knew how turned on Liv was right now and didn't want to make her wait.

Liv lay down, but made a small noise of dismay when Juliette got off the bed.

"Don't worry, you'll like this. I got you a wedding present. Well, us, really – I got us a wedding present."

"Well, now I'm intrigued."

Juliette had made sure it was charged before they left. She pulled out the purple rabbit ear vibrator and turned it on.

Liv's eyes widened. "That looks fucking fantastic."

"You mentioned that you've never tried one of these before. I was curious. The thing is great."

"You've tried it already? Our wedding gift – how dare you!" Liv's feigned indignation was somewhat ruined by how breathy and needy her voice sounded.

"I had to make sure it was up to scratch before using it on my wife."

"Fine. Just get that thing in me already."

"With pleasure."

Juliette ran her fingers through Liv's vulva first,

testing to see that she was wet enough for the rather large dildo. She needn't have worried; Liv was soaked.

Liv cried out as Juliette pressed the dildo into her. She put her feet up on the bed, bending her knees and using the leverage to thrust her hips forward. Juliette looked down and made a small adjustment, ensuring that the rabbit ears were brushing Liv's clit on every stroke.

The difference was immediately apparent in Liv's increasingly urgent cries.

"Talk to me," Liv begged.

"You're gonna come so hard, baby. I'm your wife, now. Your pussy belongs to me and only me. You're going to come for me. Do it, Liv. Come, now!"

Liv came so hard that her pussy almost expelled the dildo. Juliette put some muscle into keeping it inside, thrusting harder and faster than before, drawing Liv's orgasm out until she began to worry that she had been right about Liv's scream attracting security.

Thankfully, no one came – except for Liv. She definitely came.

Juliette withdrew the dildo and turned it off before folding herself into Liv's arms. Liv sighed contentedly. "If that's what every night as your wife is like, I may not live for long."

"I'm not going to fuck you to death... only until you're on your last legs, and then I will revive you with a kiss."

"Sounds good to me," Liv murmured. They were quiet for a few minutes before Liv spoke again. "I never woke up, you know."

"What?"

"You remember when you came to me, that night in the airport?"

"How can I forget?"

"I thought at the time that it must be a dream. I hoped for nothing more other than that I never woke up. I never did."

"If this is a dream, then I hope I never wake up either. But I don't think we need to worry. It's not a dream – it's simply a waking paradise. A happy ending, like the happily ever afters in love stories."

"You deserve your happily ever after. I'm so proud of you, Juliette. And I'm so glad that I get to share your happy ending with you."

"I love you, Liv."

"I love you too."

Juliette was already planning her next paint-ing. This one would be inspired by the peace and beauty of Liv's sleeping face. She was exhausted, but she wanted to stay up a little while longer, to watch as Liv drifted off. It was a sight she could never get enough of, and had yet to translate perfectly onto a canvas.

Juliette would keep trying, though she suspected that painting Liv's true beauty was a pointless endeavor, because no picture – no matter how skillful the artist – could come close to encapsulating the glory that was Juliette's wife.

That didn't mean she would stop attempting it. Juliette would spend the rest of her life loving and appreciating Liv, and reveling in the marvelous fact that somehow, Liv felt the same way about her.

If this truly was a dream, then Liv was right. Juliette never wanted to wake up.

FREE BOOK

I really hope you enjoyed this story. I loved writing it.

I'd love for you to get my FREE book- Her Boss- by joining my mailing list. Just click on the following link or type into your web browser: https://BookHip.com/MNVVPBP

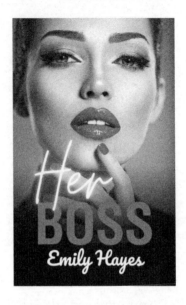

Meg has had a huge crush on her hot older boss for some time now. Could it be possible that her crush is reciprocated? https:// BookHip.com/MNVVPBP

ALSO BY EMILY HAYES

If you enjoyed this one, dive into the next of the super popular CEO Series, Thawing the CEO. Can single mom Emma melt the icy facade of her CEO boss, or will their forbidden attraction thaw more than just her boss's heart? Find out in this sizzling romance that blurs the lines between professional and personal.

mybook.to/CEO9

Printed in Great Britain
by Amazon

39834326R00096